To The Overland Trail
(Buckskin Chronicles 8)

B. N. Rundell

To The Overland Trail (Buckskin Chronicles 8)

B. N. Rundell

**WOLFPACK
PUBLISHING**
— EST 2013 —

Wolfpack Publishing
6032 Wheat Penny Avenue
Las Vegas, NV 89122

Print Edition ISBN 978-1-64119-031-2

Dedication

During the writing of this book, my wife and I celebrated our 51st wedding anniversary. Although the time of our meeting seems like only yesterday, the surprising thought is how my better half has managed to navigate the challenges of the last half-century. At one time, I thought I would retire at 35, be a millionaire, and die at the ripe old age of 50. But that was a day-dream of a tow-headed youngster lying in the grass and watching the clouds drift across the blue Colorado sky. But if I could dream again, it would be to have a loving wife, beautiful children, and a great life and that's exactly what I've enjoyed. A dream come true to be dreamed again and every precious moment, a gift from God, to be savored all over again while I lay in the grass and hold hands with my love and watch the clouds drift slowly by across the blue skies of Colorado.

Chapter One

Bull

THE SUN PRIED ITS WAY through the narrow crack between the logs of the stable where Talon sought to rid himself of the restless night. With one eye open to greet the morning, he sat up to escape the merciless ray of the sunrise that was intent on painting the Eastern sky with its palette of oranges and pinks. Without a cloud in the sky to shield the reluctant young man from the coming day, he rose from his bed of hay and blankets to stretch to his full height of just over six feet. Stretching his arms out, his broad shoulders bunched under his buckskin shirt as he yawned and waved his arms to get his circulation going in his long limbs.

He ran his fingers through his dark copper hair and felt his face for the growth of whiskers. Still too young to have much of a beard, he kept himself well-shaved and groomed as a matter of preference and to please his wife of just a few weeks. He stepped out of the hay-filled stall with his bedroll over his shoulder and his two rifles and scabbards under his left arm. Seeing the stage station hostler entering the building he greeted him with, "Howdy Jake, you're up early ain'tcha?"

1

The brawny black man with high water britches held up by galluses stretched over muscular shoulders grinned at the young man and answered, "Nossuh, but youse a gittin' up kinda late. You bettuh git to da table if'n youse wantin' some vittles."

Talon chuckled and replied, "I'm definitely wantin' some, that's for sure. I'm hungry 'nuff to eat 'bout half a cow!"

He sat his gear down beside the wash bench and splashed a double handful of water on his face and reached for the well-used towel that hung nearby on a wooden peg in the log wall of the station. The North Platte station was a home station and provided sleeping quarters for the Jehu or stage driver and the Shotgun and accommodations for the travelers, although Talon preferred the solitude of a hay-filled stall in the barn. Situated on the East bank of the North Platte River and surrounded by tall cottonwoods and an abundance of willows, it was an oasis in the middle of nowhere.

Stages coming from the West had traveled well over a hundred miles from Fort Bridger, the last pleasant stop on the East bound trail, and the appearance of trees and green grass on the banks of the river were a welcome sight to both travelers and horses. The station itself was a well-built log structure of two stories and several rooms, the largest of which was the central dining room that could easily accommodate twelve hungry travelers per sitting.

Talon reached for his rifles and bedroll and turned to the door of the station but had to step back for a man-mountain to exit the building. With his head bowed and his face covered with a floppy felt hat, the big man stomped from the station and passed Talon without a glance. Talon paid little attention to the big man's leaving and stepped into the station.

Letting his eyes adjust to the dim light, he paused by the door, sat his rifles and bedroll down and stepped to the table to join the remaining few that were finishing their meal. He no sooner sat down and a matronly woman set a plate full of food before him and poured a cup full of Arbuckles. Looking down at his plate, he was pleased to see several biscuits peeking from under steaming gravy and sausage. Talon didn't hesitate to make short work of the fine smelling and good tasting breakfast and was soon pushing himself back from the table when he heard, "There's more if you want it!" from the woman that served him earlier.

"No thanks m'am, I'm afraid if I stayed to eat as much as I'd like, not only would I be too heavy to lift myself up on the stage, they'd probly' leave me anyway!"

She laughed at his response, wiped her hands on her apron and waved him on with, "Oh, go on with you now, you sweet talkin' devil you!"

Talon grinned broadly and picked up his rifles and bedroll as he exited the station. The hostler was just finishing harnessing the horses and hooking up their trace chains as Talon stretched up and put his rifles in the front boot leaning them against the box seat. He stepped on the front hub and with one foot atop the front wheel, he climbed up to the seat. Moving his Spencer and scabbard to the top of the coach he hooked the strap over the rail. His coiled black snake bullwhip rested easily around the butt of the Henry that stood beside his knee.

The young man had always gone well armed and now carried a Remington Army revolver on his left hip, butt forward. Resting between his shoulder blades and out of sight under his buckskin shirt was a scabbarded Bowie knife and tucked into his belt on his right hip was a tomahawk. This had been his normal equipage from his youth, as he became expert with each of the weapons he naturally added them to his usual attire.

A soft-spoken and unassuming young man, Talon Thompsett was well-experienced as a Shotgun on the Overland Stage line, gaining a wealth of knowledge in a short time under the tutelage of his friend and mentor, Mac MacGillicutty, the first driver he'd rode with earlier in the year. He was now ready for his return trip to LaPorte and to the waiting arms of his wife, Ginny, one of the two girls that were the subjects of a rescue from a raiding band of Cheyenne dog soldiers. Still newlyweds, the two-young people took advantage of every opportunity to be together and Talon knew she would be waiting at the end of his two-day return journey.

The stage rocked to the side as a massive paw grabbed at the rail beside the seat and the man-mountain hefted himself up to stare at the young man over the edge of the seat. The pause was short and with a grumble the big man wrestled his bulk into the seat and reached down to grab the lines for the team. He turned and looked at Talon with a grunt and said, "So you're 'sposed to be the Shotgun on this trip?"

Talon gave a single nod of his head in response without speaking.

"Cain't you talk?"

"Yup."

The big man leaned over and with his right hand that was the size of a bear's paw, folded Talon's ear forward and grunted. "Ummhumm, just like I thot, still wet behind the ears." Talon didn't respond choosing not to provoke this man that was easily twice his size. He'd heard stories about Bull and wasn't anxious to get on his bad side. He was known to be able to crush a man with a bear hug as easily as he could stomp his chest into the ground like a stampeding buffalo.

There was no fear on the part of Talon, but he had often been taught by his father that discretion is the better part of valor and a man can learn a lot more by listening and watching than he could by provoking a fight or argument. Talon leaned back against the seat and put one foot on the front edge of the boot and crossed his legs as he leaned back giving the impression of comfort and lack of concern.

The driver grabbed the lines with both hands and slapped the team on their rumps and hollered, "Ándele!" to get the stage started on the way.

"So, what'syur name boy?" asked the big man without looking at Talon.

4

"Talon," he answered.

The driver gave a quick glance toward the lean figure that appeared somewhat slouched in his seat and back to the road as he said, "You the one that went after them injuns?"

"Yup."

"You don't say! As I recall they said you went alone after them Cheyenne that took them wimmin, that right?"

"Yup."

"An' you brung 'em back all by yoreself?"

"Yup, ceptin' there was a boy with 'em too. And after we got to the stage road, we came on the stage with Mac," answered Talon without elaboration.

"Yeah, I know Mac, good man."

"Yup."

"Well, sonny boy, I'm called Bull."

"That whatchur Momma named you?" asked Talon.

"Humph, no. She named me Buford Beauregard Blackstone and the last man that laughed at that name is still looking for his teeth! After the first fight, folks started callin' me Bull and it just seemed to fit, so that's what I'm known as now." The big man laughed and his wide grin wrinkled his cheeks as his big belly bounced with the laughter.

Talon relaxed and uncrossed his arms and leaned forward to scan the road ahead. They were traveling over sage brush flats with the low rolling hills dotted with buffalo grass, random pinion and cedar trees, and clumps of sage. He watched as a long-legged jack rabbit scampered from one clump to another seeking to hide from the prowling coyote. In the distance to the East he spotted a small herd of antelope lazily grazing on the low growing gramma. The sun was in their faces but both men welcomed the warmth and relished the slight breeze that carried the scent of dust and sage. Their next stop would be Pass Creek.

To The Overland Trail

Chapter Two

Wagons

THE AUTUMN OF 1864 was a time of conflict in the West and more so in Colorado Territory and the territory to the North, known as Idaho territory and Nebraska territory. Thousands of emigrants were moving to the West to claim homesteads in the new Oregon territory and many ended their journey and settled in the newly founded Colorado territory. With this influx of settlers, the government began restricting the lands of the natives by claiming much of their land for settlers and moving the natives onto reservations.

This caused considerable conflict between the whites and the Cheyenne, Arapaho, Ute and Sioux peoples, whose young warriors chose to fight instead of surrender to the encroachment of the white man. Although most of the conflicts during the fall of 1864 were between remote settlements or wagon trains and the Indians, none of the battles rose to the level of outright war, at least not in comparison to the ongoing Civil War being waged in the East.

Talon was no stranger to Indian fighting, having been raised on a remote ranch in the middle of Indian country between traditional territories of the Ute and the Cheyenne. He chose to leave the ranch and strike out on his own after his twin brother, Tyrell, won the heart of their childhood sweetheart. Although it seemed like a lifetime ago, it was only the springtime of this same year when he drove a small herd of cattle from the ranch to LaPorte and Camp Collins to earn his stake.

Shortly after that he was hired by the Overland Stage Line by the founder of the line, Ben Holladay, when he witnessed Talon handle himself in an attempted robbery and the recovery of his property from the perpetrators. Although young, he had attained the stature of a man and conducted himself accordingly and easily stepped into the role of Shotgun for the stage line. After single-handedly rescuing two young women and a boy from the Cheyenne Dog soldiers that had attacked a wagon train, Talon married Ginny, the more outspoken of the two women.

Although Bull was a big man and was assumed to be somewhat of a dullard, such was not the case. He did allow others to presume he was somewhat hindered in his intellect, but he knew their presumption, though wrong, would give him an advantage in any situation. Most also assumed he was a bully of sorts, but the truth be known, he was as tender hearted as they come.

But now he considered this young whippersnapper he seemed to be saddled with as a Shotgun. With the constant threat of Indian attack and the occasional attempted robbery, it was important to Bull to have a capable sidekick on the seat with him and he wasn't sure that this youngster would measure up.

As he absent-mindedly maneuvered the team along the dusty stage road, he considered what he had heard about the boy and his recent experience with the Indians. The story was that the young man had struck out on his own and by himself to find and rescue two women and a boy that had been taken from a wagon train and he had succeeded. And against the well-known proven warriors of the dog soldier society of the Cheyenne people, this was no easy task. If what he had heard was true, then maybe the boy would do to ride the river with, but time would tell. He just hoped he didn't have to pay the price for the boy's initiation into the difficulties of the trail.

The easy rocking motion of the stage was countered by the rough road with the many ruts and rocks as well as the dust from the hooves of the six-up team as they stretched out in the ground eating canter. There were only three passengers for this leg of the trip, all men, but a considerable load of mail bags and other parcels. With the ongoing settlement in the Oregon territory and the continuing gold rush in California, the load of mail was considerable. It was the contract with the government to carry the mail that made the line profitable.

Talon sat almost mindlessly and rocked with the stage as he surveyed the countryside for any sign of danger but there was little to break the monotony of the sage, grass, occasional dark green of scattered clusters of stunted cedar and pinion trees, and a whole lot of nothing. With eyes that continually searched for movement, the occasional jackrabbit or coyote did not go unnoticed.

The fall colors were painting the mountainside of the nearby Elk Mountain. Talon enjoyed the brilliant golds of the aspen intermingled with the deeper reds and oranges of the buckbrush. The cooler evenings were harbingers of the coming winter but it was a time enjoyed by Talon and his family on the ranch. He remembered the preparations for winter, the gathering of the cattle and storing of fresh cut hay, the cutting of firewood and the canning of the fall harvest from the garden, all things done together as a family in preparation for a long winter.

The pace of life seemed to slow with the coming of winter as animal and people alike prepared for their hibernation and it was a time that Indian attacks seemed to taper off and the influx of emigrants dwindled. Yes, fall was his favorite time of year.

He was surprised to see a snake of white topped wagons emerging from the foothills as this was a sight usually reserved for the spring and early summer, but this year there were many trains, even late departing ones, headed to the promised land in Oregon territory. As he watched, he counted over forty wagons, most pulled by horses or mules and a few with oxen. He shook his head at the stubborn determination of the many pilgrims foolish enough to undertake such a journey this time of year. He knew they would probably get snowed in somewhere and need to hole up for the winter, if they survived long enough. He shook his head and muttered, "Pilgrims!"

"Ain't that the truth!" answered Bull. "Ain't got the sense God gave a prairie dog! They'll probably get out past Fort Bridger and end up stranded in some blizzard. They'd be better off just stayin' south, maybe Denver city or someplace an' waitin' fer Spring, but they're so afraid of somebody else gettin' the land or the gold claim before 'em, they'll risk their lives for it all. Dumb, just plain dumb!"

Talon was a little surprised at this outburst from the big man, but it showed him another side of the Jehu and he began to realize that what others told him about Bull might not be all there was to the man. As he thought about it, he nodded his head and answered, "You're right about that."

It was a common understanding that the stages had the right-of-way on the Overland trail and most would give way to the faster traveling stage, but this train thought they had first right and refused to move from the road. As Bull pulled the stage to a stop in front of the first wagon, he noticed a pair of men riding up on horseback to see what was the hold up. The manner of the bigger of the two men told of his assumed authority and Talon and Bull judged him to be the wagon master.

He hollered at Bull, "What do you think yore doin'? Get that thing outta the way so we can keep goin'!"

Bull remained calm as he said, "I guess you didn't know, this here is the Overland Stage road and the stage has the right-of-way. So, how 'bout you movin' your wagons aside so we can pass?" Bull's deep voice was matter-of-fact with no give or compromise suggested.

"Git that thing outta the way, I'm tellin' you! We got 43 wagons and we ain't movin' for no stage! Now, if you don't move, we'll move you!" threatened the wagon master.

Talon watched both men and leaned slightly forward with the coach gun across his lap but with his Remington revolver readily accessible. His bullwhip hung from his hand between his knees as he watched both men.

"You don't really want to do that," cautioned Bull, "anyone that touches my team will have me to reckon with," he said as he breathed deep and rolled his shoulders back. The warning was unmistakable and the wagon master spurred his horse forward. The second man let his hand drop to his sidearm and in an instant Talon's whip caught the man's hand and split the back of his hand with the lash.

The wagon master turned to see the black snake bull whip lash out again and slap the rump of his mount causing the horse to jump forward and tuck his head between his feet and kick at the clouds with his hind feet. Both men were startled and the big wagon master grabbed for his saddle horn but found only air as he was somersaulted over the head of his horse. Before he hit the ground, Talon's lash found the rump of the second man's horse and it took off at a full run with the rider grabbing leather for dear life.

Talon casually coiled his whip as the wagon master pushed himself up to his knees and struggled to stand erect. Bull fought to keep a straight face as he instructed the wagon master, "Now would be a good time to signal your wagons to pull aside."

The angry and dusty wagon master grumbled as he turned to the wagons and with a wave of his arms he motioned for the wagons to pull to the side. The stage remained standing as the wagons pulled to the side and began moving past the stage. When the road was clear before him, Bull slapped the rumps

11

of the team with the leads and they leaned into the traces and started the stage as they resumed the familiar canter. As they cleared the last wagon, Bull turned to Talon and said, "You're purty handy with that thing. You just might do to have around."

"Yup," answered Talon with a grin splitting his face.

Pass Creek station came into view as the stage neared the foothills below Elk Mountain. This was just a swing station and would avail the travelers of nothing more than a short stop long enough for a walk to the outhouse and a stretch of their legs. The station was nothing more than a one room log house with a sod roof and a large barn and corrals for the teams.

As they approached two men came from the house with one going to the corrals for the fresh team. The station keeper took the reins of the leaders and started to remove the harness and undo the trace chains. He was no sooner finished with the trace chains and the hostler was ready with the fresh team.

Bull and Talon dropped from the driver's box and stretched their legs with a short walk around the stage. The three passengers, two peddlers and one rancher, made their trips to the outhouse and were returning when the rancher approached Bull and asked, "What was all that about when we passed the wagon train? When I saw that one fella hangin' on to leather with his horse takin' off, I thought there was gonna be trouble."

"Nah, no trouble. Just had to give the wagon master a little schoolin' on Western etiquette!" answered Bull. The rancher looked at him with a quizzical expression that told of his surprise at the big man using such words as 'etiquette' but he chose to let the matter drop and climbed back into the stage. Bull just grinned at the retreating rancher and proceeded to climb back into the driver's box and prepare for the next leg of the trip. Rattlesnake canyon beckoned just past the stage station and it was not the safest part of the journey.

Chapter Three

Rollin'

PASS CREEK STATION was nestled at the junction of Pass Creek and Rattlesnake Creek. The stage road crossed Pass Creek at a shallow gravel bedded crossing that did little more than give the horses a fresh drink of clear mountain water. After leaving the station, the road followed the South side of Rattlesnake Creek into the canyon of the same name. The hills on either side rose sharply from the creek bed and tenuously held clusters of boulders large enough to flatten the stage should they lose their uncertain footing.

Timber was more prevalent throughout the steep ravines that cascaded down the steep hillsides, the same ravines that shed spring runoff waters with a vengeance. But the greenery was a pleasant change from the dusty sagebrush flats although the deep green of the juniper and cedar provided hiding places for possible Indian attacks. Small clusters of Aspen and Cottonwood stubbornly clung to their golden leaves as they rattled in the breeze as the stage passed.

If it was just a sight-seeing trip, the journey would be very enjoyable, but this canyon was notorious as a favorite of the

Indians and their attacks on the stage. Talon was vigilant as he scanned the rocky escarpments and the clusters of trees for any indication of danger.

Bull also repeatedly searched the steep hillsides for Indians or any other impending threats. The canyon walls echoed back the rattle of hooves and thunder of the passing stage. The road that followed the twisting stream took a narrow turn to the right around a sharp shoulder of stone and caused Bull to slow the team to a walk as they negotiated the curve. Before the team and stage were straightened out, Bull leaned back on the lines and hollered to the team, "Whoa up thar, whoa, now."

Before them lying across the road was a large ponderosa that covered the width of the road with its top dipping into the waters of the creek. Talon searched the hillsides as he reached back for his Spencer. The big rifle had greater range than the Henry and held sixteen rounds in the tube fed magazine and Talon knew the Spencer would be better suited for any enemy high up on the steep hillsides. As the team pranced impatiently, Bull said, "You keep watch, I'll move that tree."

Talon looked at the big pine that blocked the road and back at Bull and said, "You're gonna move that by yourself? Don't you want me to help you?"

"You help by keepin' any Indians off my back," then motioning toward the tree, "I think that was cut down just to stop the stage. Watch yourself."

Bull stepped down from the stage and started for the tree just as an arrow whispered past Talon's shoulder. He immediately spotted the Indian nocking another arrow and without hesitation he pulled up the Spencer and fired. The resounding boom of the big gun echoed through the canyon and was followed by the scream of the Indian as the massive .52 caliber slug smashed his breastbone against his back and knocked him off the huge boulder.

Talon searched for another target as the report of a rifle sounded and a puff of grey smoke revealed the location of the shooter. Talon had his left foot on the edge of the driver's boot and rested his elbow on his knee. He saw the shoulder of the shooter and quickly took a bead on the exposed flesh, squeezed off his shot and was rewarded with another scream as the slug tore through the shoulder of the Indian.

Two others started down the steep hillside thinking it would take time for Talon to reload but were surprised when the Spencer barked again and the first of the attackers did a somersault down the hill with half his head gone. The shot surprised the second attacker who paused in his step long enough for Talon to jack another round and take aim. His shot tore through the throat of the warrior splattering flesh, blood and bone across the boulders behind him.

Talon didn't know how many attackers were in the war party, but when they realized they had already lost four of their number in just the first couple of minutes, they thought their medicine was bad and quickly disappeared behind the trees. Soon, the clatter of hoofs bounced from the canyon walls signaling the departure of the remaining Indians. The dust cloud told of their flight over a saddle between the hills.

Talon looked to Bull and saw the big man stoop at the stump end of the ponderosa. He noticed the size of the trunk was easily two feet across, but Bull bent his knees and reached his massive arms around the trunk. He slowly straightened his legs, lifting the trunk of the tree as he did, side-stepped a short distance and dropped the tree. It had only moved a few feet and Bull stood with hands on his hips and breathing deeply as he rested a moment.

Talon was mesmerized as he watched the big man repeat his steps again and again until the massive tree was lying alongside the road at the top of the creek bank. Bull sat on a sizable boulder at the edge of the road and rested for just a couple of minutes then stood and walked back to the stage. Talon looked at Bull and back at the tree and noted the tree was easily three times the size of the man at twenty feet tall and with a trunk diameter of two feet. Never before had he

15

witnessed such a display of strength and he looked at Bull and just shook his head in wonder.

As Bull settled himself on the driver's seat, he looked at Talon and said, "Not bad, four shots, four killed."

"Well, I thought about just waitin' on you, I thought you were just gonna throw that tree at 'em. But they got a little anxious so I thought I'd try to discourage 'em a mite."

Bull looked at the young man and let a slow grin creep across his face as he replied, "Yeah, you did that alright. Course if them worthless bluecoats from the 11th Ohio were doin' their job, there wouldn't a been any injuns hereabout to cause the problem. They ain't nuthin' but a worthless bunch o' drunks," he muttered as he shook his head. He started the team with a slap of the lines and an "Andele!"

As the stage broke from the tree lined roadway and into the wide grassy clearing, the many structures of Fort Halleck became visible. It was the largest complex between LaPorte and Fort Bridger with stables large enough for two hundred horses, two buildings for company quarters, officers' quarters, storehouses, a sutler's building, a bake house, jail and even a hospital. The stage station was beside the stables and Bull brought the stage to a stop in front of the station. This was a home station and would have a meal for everyone. While the hostler and his helper took care of the team, Bull, Talon and the passengers made their way into the station in anticipation of a good meal.

As they were seated along both sides of the table, the station keeper with a dirty apron around his front began placing the food before them. A big platter of trout caught their attention right off and it was followed by a plate of biscuits accompanied by a jar of buffalo berry jelly. A large bottle of 'Valley Tan' whiskey was set at the end of the table alongside a big pot of hot coffee. Bull didn't hesitate to fill his plate with trout and biscuits and grabbed the coffee pot to pour out a cupful of the black brew. Talon copied the driver but was unable to match his appetite as Bull finished two plates full before Talon emptied his first plate.

Talon noticed Bull avoid the whiskey, for which he was thankful, but the peddlers readily filled their cups with the rank smelling potion. As it seemed to fall in clumps into the cups, the dark turbid liquid reminded Talon of the contents of the brass spittoons emptied into the alleyways behind the bars in LaPorte.

Both peddlers choked and coughed as they downed their first drought and the rancher laughed at their response. When they looked at him he said, "I heard it said that stuff was made from horned toads and rattlesnakes! But of course, that can't be true cuz we ain't got no horned toads in these hyar parts!" as he laughed at them.

Bull chimed in with, "I knew a bull whacker that drank that stuff and he said after it got to workin' on him he figgered he could whip all the Indians on the plains and any of the bull-whackers that had ever talked back to him."

Everyone laughed as the peddlers continued to cough and choke on the spirits. The station keeper stood with hands on his hips as he said, "They ain't nothin' wrong with this whiskey, 'ceptin' the only fault is, it ain'tny good!"

Talon turned to the station keeper and asked, "I've heard folks startin' to call this place Whiskey Gap, is that stuff why?"

The station keeper laughed and said, "No, not hardly young feller. Ya see, here a while back a wagon train come through and there was this feller that had a few barrels of 'frontier whiskey' and started sellin' it to them sojer boys for $5 a canteen full. Wal, after most of 'em got good an' drunk, even the night guard, ol' Major O'Farrell got so mad, he ordered the rest of 'em that weren't drunk to search the wagons and find the whiskey and destroy it.

Wal, you know ain't none of 'em too bright, but they found the whiskey and rolled the barrels out and busted 'em open. Problem was, where they busted them barrels was right above the spring and it all ran down into the water supply for the fort.

Wal' they did ever'thing they could to save some of it, even lay down on the ground and lapped it up. It took three days for all them sojer boys to sober up! Heeheehee . . . so, ever since then, folk's a been callin' it Whiskey Gap." The station keeper continued to giggle and laugh at the memory of the event as he cleared the table and bid good bye to the travelers.

The afternoon would be a long one with stops at three more swing stations before reaching the home station of Big Laramie where they would spend the night. Bull was anxious to get started and hurried the passengers to the stage to load up so they could get on the way. Talon was already seated when the big man rocked the stage as he climbed aboard and started the stage moving without another word to the passengers as they sought to find their seats with the stage rocking back with the sudden start.

Bull turned to Talon and said, "I'm thinkin' we're in for some trouble 'fore we get to Big Laramie. Them injuns in the canyon probly' got some friends and I'm thinkin' they might try to hit us again. Course, there could be a totally different bunch waitin' for us too. I just got this feelin' and I ain't usually wrong 'bout these things."

Talon could tell the big man was a bit fidgety and he knew he best keep a careful watch. There had been several reports of increased Indian attacks and all the station keepers were uneasy with the stories being relayed to them. Talon knew it was something to be concerned about and he was disturbed. He looked off to the distance and began to pray that God would see them through. Talon was a man of prayer and knew the best thing he could do would be to earnestly seek the presence and protection of his God.

Chapter Four

Council

THE SOMBER FACES OF the council members told of the gravity of the time and the concern for the future of the people. The council had been called to consider the proposal of the blue coats at Fort Lyon and their offer of peace and safety.

These were the leaders of the Southern Cheyenne and the Southern Arapaho that had allied themselves together and shared the vast territory that had been ceded to the white government under the treaty of Fort Wise. But that treaty had been repeatedly broken by the whites with the thousands of emigrants that crossed their lands and took the buffalo and other game so necessary for the survival of the people.

Now the whites wanted to meet again and the people asked the council to make the decision. Gathered at the council were leaders of the bands of Cheyenne, Black Kettle, chief of the Wutapai, Yellow Wolf and Big Man of the Hevhaitaniu, War Bonnet of the Oivimana, White Antelope and One Eye of the Hisiometanio. The Suhtai clan and the Heviqxnipahis clan were represented by chief Sand Hill. The Arapaho chief, Left Hand, stood alone for his people.

Black Kettle started the council with the lighting of the pipe, offering it to the four directions, the sky and the earth, then passing it to Yellow Wolf and on around the circle of the council. When the smoking of the pipe was completed, Black Kettle began, "Word has come from the white man Evans about a parley for peace. They want us to meet with them at Fort Lyon to discuss this peace. I have not answered him."

The chiefs looked from one to the other and Yellow Wolf spoke, "Have they said what this peace means, that we do not have, or is different than what was promised before?"

"Why is this different from the broken promises from other treaties? They cannot be trusted! They have taken our land and continue to kill our people, why should we meet with them?" demanded chief, One Eye. Several of the others nodded their heads and murmured their agreement.

"Lean Bear and Star agreed to their terms and they and their people were slaughtered by the blue coats!" shouted Yellow Wolf. Again, the agreement and anger came from several of the circle by their talking and beating war clubs on the ground in front of them.

White Antelope raised his hands for quiet and began to speak, "What you say is true and it is a sad day when we lose any of our people, but the numbers of the whites are more than we can count and some say as many as the stars of the heavens. The numbers of our people, even though we have allied with the Arapaho and some of the Sioux, are not enough to fight against this great number. Our Dog Soldiers continue to fight and kill many of the whites, but for every one that is killed, two hands full more come. What can we do against so many?"

Heads nodded and many grumbled but several moments passed before another spoke. War Bonnet began with a low voice that demanded attention and quiet, "We are old," as he motioned around the circle of elders and chiefs, "and we have had our time. The herds of buffalo were great and other game plentiful, our lodges were warm with beautiful women and laughing children and time was good to us. Then came the white man and his sickness and many of our people, young and old died. Then more came and took our lands and the blue coats killed many of our people. Our young men have gone to battle and taken many scalps and plunder, but they have not defeated the white man. We do not have the weapons or the warriors to fight and win and if we cannot win, we will all die including our women and children. If we make peace, perhaps our young people will live and our people will continue."

There was sadness evident on every face as each one realized the truth of what the respected War Bonnet had spoken. Several stared at the council fire and thought about their future and if there would be a life for their people. No one else spoke for some time and Black Kettle proposed, "We," as he motioned to everyone present and looking to the lodges of the encampment, "will go to this fort Lyon and see if this peace and safety the white man speaks of will be ours." He stood and turned away from the council and started for his lodge. At this signal, the others also rose and left to prepare for the journey before them.

Black Kettle was resting on his favorite buffalo robe when a scratch at the opening of his lodge told of someone asking entrance. He responded with "Enter."

Two warriors of the Dog Soldiers ducked their heads as they stepped through the doorway of the buffalo hide lodge and at the direction of Black Kettle, seated themselves across from him. The chief said, "Welcome to my lodge, Black Wolf and Red Hawk. You bring me news of your band?"

"We came to learn what the council has decided about the white man's talk of peace," spoke Black Wolf. He was known as a war leader for the Dog Soldiers and had led his warriors on many raids against the white men and their wagon trains and against the many stage stations. He was a respected and even feared leader among the Cheyenne and Sioux that made up his band of Dog Soldiers.

"We have decided to go to this Fort Lyon and seek after peace," answered Black Kettle.

"Bah! You've done that before and we still do not have peace. The white men continue to take our land and kill our buffalo. We should make war on them and drive them from our lands!" he declared angrily.

"We know this is what you and the other Dog Soldiers believe, but we, the elders and chiefs of our people, believe we must try again for peace. There are too many of the white men and our weapons and numbers are no match for the many blue coats and their weapons."

Red Hawk waved his arms and said, "We have taken many of these weapons in our raids and we will take more! Their scalps decorate our shields and our lances and we will drive them away!"

As Black Kettle looked at the two angry warriors he wondered if they were trying to convince him or themselves. He remembered the times in the past when he was just as anxious for battle and the glory that came with victory, but he also thought of the many friends that now walked on the other side and would never again know the love of a woman or the laughter of a child.

He hung his head in sadness and spoke, "Each man must do as he believes in his heart is right for him and those that follow him. I too was once like you, but that was in a time when the buffalo were more than both the people and the white man. But now, that is not so, and we must think of the future generations of our people, our children must live for the people to continue."

Black Wolf stood and looked at the venerated chief and remembered the many stories told of his battles and victories. This man had been his idol from childhood and now to see him as an old man and weak gave him pause. But he thought, *I must carry on the fight, for our people to live, we must drive the white men out of our lands.*

He looked at Black Kettle and said, "Grandfather, I remember the stories of when you had to lead our people against the words of the council and became a great chief. Now it is I who must do the same. The Dog Soldiers will continue to make war against the white men until they are driven from this land."

The old chief looked at the eager warriors and nodded his head in understanding but a sadness filled his heart with the realization that their cause, though noble, was unwinnable. But he also knew these young warriors would not be dissuaded and their determination would bring them honor as well as death. He raised his hand in dismissal and the two men nodded in agreement and left the lodge.

Black Kettle led the procession of almost 800, mostly Southern Cheyenne and some Arapaho under Chief Left Hand, on the short journey to the fort situated on the eastern plains of Colorado Territory. They had been promised provisions and protection by governor Evans but when they arrived, the provisions were not forthcoming.

With additional promises, the people of the Cheyenne and Arapaho were relocated away from the fort into the Big Sandy Creek area and dispersed into many different camps. Several of the tribal warriors did not agree with the decision of the council and refused to surrender to the authorities choosing instead to either ally themselves with the Dog Soldiers or make their own camps away from the others.

The chiefs had been told to fly the American flag and a white flag beneath it to show their agreement to the peace terms. Black Kettle willingly set the example and when the village was settled, proudly raised the flags over his lodge. His village was one of the larger with just over 200 men, women and children in the almost seventy lodges.

As the village settled into its usual routines, Black Kettle observed his people and smiled with pride as they seemed happy and safe, with children playing and women busy at their many tasks. Several ponies were tethered by the lodges in anticipation of hunts in this new land. Old men rested against the willow back rests and surveyed the village. It was a peaceful scene.

Chapter Five

Laramie

WHISKEY GAP QUICKLY faded in the distance as the stage rumbled toward the East with the towering Elk Mountain and its buffalo hump shape to the right of the stage road. Bull had spoken of his uneasiness and instinct of a possible attack and Talon continued his vigilance searching the flats to the left and the sloping hillside to his right. The thick timber of the mountain could hide any number of attackers and he focused most of his attention scanning the tree line for any sign of danger. He sat the coach gun butt down beside the scabbard that held his Henry, stretched his arms out and yawned widely. Bull looked sideways at his Shotgun and asked, "Are you gettin' sleepy already? We ain't been on the trail that long."

"Nah, just needin' some air that ain't half dust, is all," replied Talon.

"Hah! You need all that dust, that'll put some weight in yore backside and keep you in the seat!"

"Hummmph, don't need any o' that. Say, what've you been hearin' 'bout all these Indian attacks? Ain't the army 'sposed to be doin' sumpin' 'bout it?" asked Talon.

"Problem is, just like that bunch back at Fort Halleck, they don't wanna do nuthin' but lay around and get drunk. Course there's them sojers with the 1st Colorado that fought with them Rebs at Glorieta Pass, but they're now under that crazy Chivington and they ain't much better. Did you know that Chivington was a minister?"

"A minister? Really?"

"Yeah, he an' the governor started a school for preachers an such," answered Bull.

"What's he gonna teach? How to kill Indians?"

Bull laughed at the remark and continued his diatribe of the man. "They say he's the one what ordered them troops to attack them villages. Seems ever' time them Cheyenne attack some white men, you know, a wagon train, a stage-stop, or ranch or whatever, ol' Chivington up and goes after a village of women an' kids. Just cain't understand somebody like that," mused the big man. "They say that even when the Injuns show they're peaceable, don't make no difference, he jist kills 'em anyway." Bull shook his head in disgust as he thought about the actions of such a man.

"No wonder the Dog Soldiers are makin' so many attacks on the stations and such. They probly just figger they're hittin' back. I guess that's usually what happens when politicians like the governor get involved in things," answered Talon.

"You got that right, boy, sure 'nuff."

Talon caught movement at the tree line and leaned forward to grab his Henry but relaxed when he saw a big bull elk pushing his harem of cows into the grassy meadow. He smiled and thought about the tasty elk steaks he had enjoyed with his family on the ranch in the Medicine Bow range. He turned to Bull and asked, "So Bull, how long you been drivin' for the Overland?"

"Near 'abouts three years now. The district manager, Overby, little runt that he was, talked me into it when he saw I was a bullwhacker with the comp'ny outta St. Louie that shipped the goods to the warehouse for the line. Tol' me I'd have better pay 'n more down time. Sounded like a good deal to me so I's just took him up on it. How 'boutchu?"

"My family has a ranch back over yonder," he motioned with his arm indicating beyond Elk Mountain, "and I thought I'd do a little adventurin' and see more of the world. Left there early this year but it seems like a lifetime ago."

The trip continued without incident with a quick stop at Elk Mountain to change teams and get back on their way. The dusty road continued to give way to the canter of the team as they rocked along and made good time covering the twenty plus miles to the next stop of Rock Creek.

Talon sat up straight as he looked at the buildings of Rock Creek Station coming into view. With the appearance of a small town, there were the buildings of the stage station and others including a large two-story blockhouse. The houses told of families that made up the townspeople supporting a store and blacksmith shop and others.

Bull pulled the stage to the front of the station and dropped the lines to the waiting hostler. The men climbed down from the driver's box and stretched their legs with a trip to the outhouse. Talon freshened up by splashing water on his face and neck and running his hands through his hair.

As he dried off with a tattered towel that hung on the pump handle, he surveyed the area and watched as a couple of boys tried to outdo one another with their slingshots as they took potshots at a squirrel on a branch of the nearby tree. Two women were seated on a bench in front of the store and fanned themselves as they chattered back and forth. Talon compared the peace and quiet of this stop to the attack in the canyon and chuckled to himself how people so near to conflict with its death and destruction can go through the day as if there was nothing more to be concerned about than the weather.

He heard Bull holler at the passengers to get aboard and he trotted back to the stage to resume his seat and responsibility. The next stretch of road across the low rolling hills and flats spanned eleven miles to the stop at Cooper Creek. Another fast change of teams had them on their way and looking forward to the final stop of the day at Big Laramie. With another quick stop at Little Laramie they continued their now southerly trek.

An area known as the Big Hollow or the Sinks had to be crossed but Bull kept the stage as close to the higher edge as possible. The depression collected large alkali deposits from the runoff alkaline water that stood and evaporated leaving the dry white powdery deposit. On a hot dry day like today the alkali swirled around the hooves of the horses and the wagon wheels causing a lingering white cloud that choked both man and animal. Everyone was relieved to see the log structures and green trees along the bank of the Laramie river that told of the Big Laramie home station where they could clean up and chow down.

When they stepped down from the stage, Bull and Talon raised a bit of a dust cloud just slapping at their clothes to rid themselves of the alkali dust. Talon used his felt hat to slap away the dust and quickly made his way to the horse trough. Dipping his hat in the water, he emptied it over his head to rinse away the grime and another hatful splashed directly on his face brought a welcome relief and gave him the first chance at clean air.

Bull followed suit and both men laughed at one another as they stood in puddles of their own making. Looking around for a towel or something to dry off with, they were interrupted by the striking of a rod on the triangle to sound the call to the table for their meal. Satisfied with just shaking off as much water as they could, they made their way into the station anticipating a good meal and hopefully followed by a good night's rest.

By any standard the meal served at the Big Laramie station was exceptional. The station keeper's wife, Mildred, had prepared a pot roast of elk with potatoes and carrots and onions from her garden. Talon used a thick slice of sourdough bread to sop up the remaining gravy after he cleaned his plate for the second time. The fresh hot coffee washed the meal down and prepared them for a thick slice of hot apple pie that was met with oohs and ahhhs from all the men.

As the men heaped praise on the cook, she smiled and nodded and waddled off to the kitchen. Talon gathered his gear and headed for the barn to find a spot for his blankets and a bit of solitude. The hostler pointed him to the loft and he found some fresh hay and a view of the valley that suited him very well.

He stretched out on his blankets and with the fading light of the setting sun, picked up his reading of the Bible in the book of John. He smiled as he remembered his mother's instructions to keep up with his reading and his praying and he pictured his red-headed mother shaking her finger at him after she hugged him good bye. He closed the book and smiled and soon drifted off to sleep.

To The Overland Trail

Chapter Six

Ginny

"WOULD YOU LOOK AT THAT! Begosh and begorra, I do believe that's a woman in them buckskins! Now what is this world comin' to when the women don't look like women and the men cain't do nuthin' 'bout it?" stated Bull as he leaned back against the lines of the team and brought the stage to a stop in front of the LaPorte station.

He was looking at the figure leaning against the post of the station porch with a Henry rifle cradled in her arms, her dark hair cascading out from under a floppy felt hat and her feminine features plainly visible beneath the well-fitted and fringed buckskins. A lazy, long-haired grey dog with floppy ears and blue eyes lay at her feet but didn't miss a thing. The woman's broad smile and confident stance dared the big man to say any more, but the words of his Shotgun stopped him before he spoke another word. "Ain't she a beauty though? I do believe she's the prettiest woman I ever saw, and that's why I married her!"

Bull caught his breath and looked at Talon to see if he was serious and did a double take toward the woman and chuckled,

"Well I'll be a monkey's uncle, the two of you do look like a pair! I guess it'd take a woman like that to make a wild one like you toe the line. Now, hop on down there and introduce me to her!" he directed with a big grin.

It took a moment for the two newlyweds to untangle themselves from one another but Talon turned and said, "Bull, I want you to meet my wife, Ginny," and turning to his wife he said, "Ginny, this is Bull, we spent the last two days getting acquainted. Don't you think we oughta have him to the house for dinner?"

Bull doffed his hat and did a slight bow and said, "Pleased to meetchu m'am, and you don't have to pay him no mind about dinner or supper or whatever you call it, I won't be imposin' on you."

"Of course, we want you to come to the house for supper. It's catch as catch can or as my momma would say, it's 'layover to catch meddlers,' but if you're hungry, we'll have the makin's and you're welcome."

"Wal, that's mighty nice of you folks, and I'd be happy to join you. I'll get cleaned up at my room at Aunt Sophies' and be right along. Talon there told me 'bout where your cabin is, so I can probly find it."

"Well, whenever you get there, we'll put the feed bucket on," said Ginny with a broad smile. She put her hand through Talon's arm and steered him toward the waiting horses tied at the rail. But before she let him mount up, she wrapped her arms around his neck and pulled his face down to hers for another lingering welcome home kiss. He didn't resist.

When she released her grip, he leaned back and said, "You sure are a welcome sight. I've been thinking about you practically every moment of this trip."

"Practically? Well I must be losing my charm. You used to think of me every minute!" and slapped him on the arm before turning to mount her horse. After securing his gear, Talon stepped into the stirrup and swung aboard the grulla mustang and whistled for the dog, Smokey, to follow.

It was a pleasant evening around the dinner table, Ginny had a beef pot roast simmering all day in the Dutch oven and quickly prepared some sourdough biscuits in another one. With a pot of mixed garden vegetables and an apple pie for desert, the men were pleasantly filled and now leaned their elbows on the table to savor the aroma of the fresh coffee that sat under their chins.

"Boy, I tell you what, you've got yourself a mighty fine home here. You sure are lucky you have such a fine wife that knows how to cook like Ginny here does. If I had a home and a wife like this, I'd probably weigh nigh unto four hunnert pounds and I'd never leave my rockin' chair. No sir, I wouldn't."

"Well, Mr. Bull, I thought sure a handsome man like you woulda been married long before now," said Ginny as she busied herself clearing the table.

"Well, missy, I did have a wife oncet. Back when I was bullwhackin' outta St. Louie, but she fell to that plague of Cholera. We'd only been hitched a couple months an' I was gone with work an' when I came back, she was gone. Just ain't had the hankerin' since then," he mused with a sad countenance overwhelming him.

"Say Bull, me'n Ginny's gonna go on a elk hunt tomorrow, you wanna come?" asked Talon, seeking to change the conversation to a more cheerful tone.

"Nah, I got some business to tend to in town, so you two go on and have a good time."

"Well, since we've got a few days off, I figgered it'd be a good time to start stokin' the larder with meat for the winter. I'm thinkin' we're gonna have a long cold winter up here."

"I think yore right 'bout that. I'm just hopin' it won't be too bad out there 'cross them plains on the way to Julesburg. That shore is miserable travelin' when the snow's a blowin' cross the road, don't like that at all, no sir," he shivered his shoulders at the thought.

The meal was finished, the conversation ebbed, and the twilight was dimming as Bull mounted up to return to town. Talon and Ginny stood arm in arm on the porch steps and waved as Bull reined his mount around to start down the trail. Talon said, "You're welcome anytime, Bull." The big man waved a hand over his shoulder as he kneed his mount to the trail. Talon and Ginny looked at each other and smiled as they turned back to enter the cabin and enjoy their time together.

Ginny led the way astride her blaze-faced sorrel gelding, followed by Talon on his Grulla, leading the pack mule. Smokey scouted the trail ahead with his stub of a tail wiggling faster than his head that moved side to side, always sniffing and looking ahead.

The sun was struggling to cast its light through the scattered cloud cover and up the narrow cut between the mountains. The chosen trail led them alongside the South bank of the Cache La Poudre river and wound its way through the intermittent fingers of fir, spruce and pine. Occasional patches of quakies still clung to the golden leaves that colored the canyon while a few of the stragglers held sway near the river to compete with the muted gold of the occasional cottonwood.

Across the river, the hillsides were carpeted in a blanket of buffalo and Indian grass with the faded blue color provided by the blue grama. Random pinion and juniper dotted the otherwise bare hillsides that were marked by clusters of jagged boulders and upthrusts of granite, all of which were covered by blue grey lichen with an occasional splash of bright orange moss. The two hunters reveled in the beauty and sucked the cool autumn air into thirsty lungs.

With a broad smile, Ginny turned to look at Talon and said, "I dreamed of this, you and me just riding together in all this beauty," as she waved her arms to her surroundings. "I love you, Talon Thompsett!"

Talon grinned as he replied, "And I love you, Mrs. Ginny Thompsett!"

The rattle of hooves on rocks, the squeak of leather, and the occasional song of birds were all that was heard as the trio of animals sauntered along the easy game trail. As they broke into a clearing and looked below them at the river, a pair of doe mule deer sprang from the willows and bounced up the hillside in front of them. Ginny quickly turned to Talon to see if they were to take the deer, but a negative nod from her husband allowed her to turn and watch the deer scamper into the trees.

Talon said, "I'd rather we get a nice elk, and if we do, it'll be all we can handle and pack out. 'Sides, those two doe are probably carryin' next spring's fawns."

Ginny smiled at the thought of the deer dropping their fawns in the spring, spotted and bashful little creatures that always caught her heart as she watched them trying their long limber legs for their first walk. She allowed her mind to wander the halls of her dreams and hopes and pictured herself with a new babe in arms.

She smiled at the idea of her being a mother and Talon being a father. For much of her life, all she ever hoped and thought she would be was a wife and mother and never in her wildest dreams did she ever think she would be riding a horse in the wilderness with her new husband and hunting for elk. She giggled to herself at the realization that life has a way of taking unexpected turns. But she was happy, and she couldn't imagine herself ever being happier than she was right now, with Talon following and her future bright.

The chatter of a squirrel brought her out of her reverie and she reined her horse to a stop as she saw a wilderness episode of life and death unfolding before her. A young lynx was circling the bottom of a towering ponderosa that held the noisy squirrel. The furry little creature twitched his tail with every chatter as he scolded the nosy but dangerous youthful lynx below him.

The big cat with pointed ears kept looking at the tasty tidbit and coughed his intentions before a quick leap took him almost six feet up the tree and with uncanny speed and dexterity he was on the limb that held the squirrel who now scampered to the end of the trembling branch and with a quick look over his shoulder, he started to leap away only to be snagged by the razor-sharp claws of the lynx.

Bringing the furry feast to his mouth, he quickly chomped down breaking the back of the squirrel and made his way to the ground to enjoy his lunch. The cat was too intent on his hunt to notice the interlopers, but a quick glance warned him of the intrusion and he scurried away into the trees, with the wooly tail of the squirrel dangling from his mouth.

Their goal was the confluence of the South Fork and the Cache La Poudre rivers. Talon knew if they followed the South Fork upstream, there were some park like clearings that offered good elk hunting, and the animals often came to water in the evening light or early morning and promised a good opportunity to take some game. Although the hunt was the practical purpose of this trek, the time together was the benefit that was treasured by both.

By mid-day they arrived at the confluence and readily found a camp site just back in the pines that would suit their plans. Dismounting, the two made their camp with practiced precision, Talon tending to the animals while Ginny arranged the packs and bedrolls. After hobbling the animals in the small clearing, Talon returned with an armful of firewood and dropped it near a large grey log they would use as a bench. He gathered some larger stones from nearby and made a fire circle for their cook-fire and pronounced everything ready as he stood with hands on hips and watched his woman take a seat on the log and give him an expression of 'really?' as she patted the log beside her for him to take a seat.

Chapter Seven

Hunt

AFTER A QUICK LUNCH of pemmican and apples, the duo started out afoot for an afternoon/evening hunt. As they followed a game trail on the west bank of the South Fork, Talon resumed his usual pattern of teaching his wife the skills of the wilderness. Every time they went into the wilds, he sought to teach her as much about their homeland and the animals as he could. He dropped to one knee and pointed at some tracks on the trail and motioned his wife to look. He asked, "Now, what kind of tracks are these?"

She knelt beside Talon and examined the tracks and said, "Those are doe, if it was a buck, they would probably be larger and splayed out a little more."

"Good, when were they made?"

She looked again at the tracks, looked around the trail and the surrounding hillside, then concluded, "Probably this morning. They look fresh with a bit of moisture compared to the rest of the trail, no debris in them, and that stone to the side was rolled over and still shows moisture on the bottom."

Smokey had returned to their side and waited for them to continue.

"Wow, I'm impressed. You didn't miss a thing," he said with pride showing on his face. He stood and started on the trail again surveying everything around them. She copied his example and scanned the trees for any movement. Being shorter than her husband, she found it easy to look through the thick timber by bending just a mite to see through the trees beneath the lower hanging branches. The carpet of pine needles now covered the trail and quieted their passing. Talon pointed out a berry bearing bush and asked, "What's that?"

"Kinnikinnick, edible but tasteless. Bears like it though."

"And what's that?" he asked pointing to a smaller cluster of green leafed brush.

"Roses, the hips are kinda like little apples and are good for you."

Continuing down the trail with Smokey in the lead, Talon stopped before reaching the edge of the trees and looked at the path before him. He motioned for Ginny to come alongside and pointed at the tracks in the way, "And those are?"

A quick look told her the maker of the marks and she immediately looked up and around as she whispered, "Bear, black bear, and they're fresh!" She clutched her rifle tightly as she continued to look around.

"But we know he's not close, or we could probably smell him and Smokey'd be raisin' a fuss. And looking at those tracks, he was in a hurry. Maybe chasing game or fleeing from something else. Maybe he got a whiff of us a bit earlier and decided to clear out," assured Talon, seeking to still his wife's nerves. He wanted her wary and vigilant, but not afraid.

"You mean bears are afraid of us?" she asked hopefully.

"Well, not so much afraid, just cautious. We are about the only enemy they have, except for the occasional grizz. Come on, we got aways to go yet, we'll be alright."

On a hunt with a seasoned hunter, both hunters would take separate positions to overlook the game trails leading to the water. However, Talon wanted Ginny to feel comfortable and safe so he kept her by his side as they came to the edge of the clearing and prepared to find a spot to make their stand. A slight promontory of rock was partially hidden by the surrounding oak brush and a couple of stunted juniper with several ponderosa and fir uphill from the jagged outcropping.

Talon motioned for Ginny to follow as he ducked back into the timber to work his way uphill to the chosen site. He indicated for her to follow his lead as he dropped to hands and knees and crawled out on the flat rock promontory to take a shooting position for their 'wait and see' approach. Smokey also crawled on his belly and lay beside them.

Lying side by side, belly down with elbows bent and chins resting on their hands, Ginny turned to look at Talon and asked, "So, we just wait for 'em to come out and get shot?"

"That's about it. See over there and down here," he motioned to the edge of the trees on both sides of the clearing, "those game trails coming from the trees are well used pathways the elk follow to get to the water. Now, if we're lucky and they're thirsty, along about dusk, we should see some of those wapiti tip-toein' outta the timber and headin' for water. When they do, you'll pick out one and we'll take him home with us."

"Wapiti? I thought we were huntin' elk?"

"That's what the Indians call 'em."

"Oh, and whatdaya mean, I'll pick one out?" she asked.

"That's right. You're gonna do the shootin'," he replied with a grin.

"Oh great! I hope you're not too hungry then."

Ginny rolled to her side and looked at Talon with a broad smile and said, "You know, if someone would have told me just a year ago that I would be lying on my belly next to my husband and hunting for elk in the mountains, I would have thought they were nuts!"

"Do you miss the city and that lifestyle?" asked Talon.

"Not a bit! But I do kinda miss my folks. I wish they were here. I wrote a letter to them but I don't know if they'll ever get it. Not knowin' where they are I just addressed it to Oregon Territory and hope they'll find it at some supply store or something."

"Well, ya never know. We carry the mail on the stages and there's lots of places along the Oregon Trail that get the mail and hold it for people that settle in the area or are coming through. Sometimes folks know others and take it to 'em," he replied trying to reassure his wife.

He remembered when she and her friends had been taken captive by the Cheyenne and her folks thought she was as good as dead so they stayed with the wagon train to Oregon Territory. He made it his personal mission to make her life without her family as good as possible, considering himself to be especially blessed to have her in his life.

A short while later, the sun dropped behind the hills to the West and the long shadows of the pines stretched across the grassy park. Talon whispered to Ginny, "Always watch where the animals are looking and be sure to not move. When you're absolutely still, you can blend in with your background and not be seen even if they're looking straight at you. But if you move, that movement will catch their eye and you'll be seen and they will disappear."

"Okay, I understand," she whispered.

Within moments of their conversation, Smokey perked his head up and let a low growl escape as Talon slowly elbowed Ginny and pointed to the far edge of the clearing on the other side of the stream. He had spotted movement and now watched as a cow elk tiptoed along the trail, carefully watching for signs of danger. Seconds later another cow, and another followed the leader into the clearing and picked up their pace as they stretched their long legs toward the waiting water.

The meandering stream had carved its snake-like path through the clearing and both banks were several paces from the tree line. As the cows dropped their heads and spread out their front legs to reach the water, another cow cleared the timber, followed closely by a young spike bull and then the herd bull with his massive antlers made his appearance. With just his front shoulders and head free of the trees, the big bull stretched his head high and sniffed the air for any warning of danger.

With the slight breeze blowing directly in the face of the hunters, they smelled the elk but their scent was not carried to the big bull. The hunters waited and as the spike bull approached the stream, he provided a broadside shot to Ginny. She snugged the Henry to her shoulder, took careful aim and squeezed off her shot. A puff of dust and the slight stagger of the young bull showed the point of impact, but he whirled and sought to retreat to the trees with the others. Ginny excitedly said to Talon, "Shoot him, shoot him, he's getting away!"

Talon already had a bead on the animal and squeezed off a quick shot and the young bull fell to his knees and plowed a slight furrow in the dirt with his chin. The rest of the small herd made their getaway and the clearing fell silent after their leaving.

Talon said, "Okay, let's go check him out and make sure he's down. Jack another round in your chamber and be ready, but let the hammer down so you won't shoot yourself in the foot."

As they approached the downed elk they waded the shallow creek and stepped up the bank. Talon was certain the animal was dead, and although Smokey was sniffing at the carcass, he nudged its hind quarters with his foot to be sure. With no movement or reaction from the animal, he said, "Okay, now, you wanna stay here and dress him, or do you wanna go back to camp and bring up the horses?"

Ginny looked at him and at the elk and said, "I think I'll just go back and get the horses and let you get all bloody from him," she said as she nodded toward the carcass.

Talon grinned and said, "Okay, but don't dilly dally cuz we're burnin' daylight." He reached for Ginny, put his arms around her waist and said, "You done right well, girl. Yes mam, I'm mighty proud of you." He pulled her to him and gave her a big hug and topped it off with a kiss.

She reached up to catch her hat that threatened to leave her head and leaning back she said, "I thought you said we were in a hurry. You keep that up and we'll never get this thing packed out," and smiled demurely at her husband. She reached down and retrieved her Henry that she had lain on the carcass and turned to start back down the trail following the dog. She quickly waded the stream, stomped her feet to get rid of excess water as Smokey shook the water from his fur, and looking back at Talon said, "I'll be back before you know it, so you better get busy on that there butcherin'!"

He waved her off and bent to start his work. Pulling his Bowie from the scabbard suspended between his shoulder blades, he rolled the bull to its back, head downhill, and slit its throat for the excess blood to escape. Then spreading the hind legs, he started the long slit from between the hind quarters to the throat to begin the gutting process.

He turned to look at the trail where Ginny disappeared thinking he'd heard something. Standing and waiting silently for a moment, the sudden sound of a gunshot startled him and when it was followed by a scream and another shot, he bent to retrieve his rifle and leaped for the stream. Another shot and another came rapidly and two more followed making Talon think there was some kind of attack by Indians or something.

His long legs carried him quickly across the clearing and into the woods. Within moments he came upon Ginny sitting at the side of the trail with her rifle standing between her knees and Smokey sitting beside her. She looked up at him as he asked, "Are you okay? What happened?"

She just pointed down the trail, unable to respond to his questions. Talon looked where she pointed and saw something black in the shadows of the pines and turned with rifle at the ready. He looked back at Ginny and then to the shadows and started carefully in that direction.

It was a mound of black fur that lay like a large boulder in the middle of the trail. The lifeless carcass of a big black bear obscured the width of the trail and Talon slowly approached. Reaching out with the barrel of his rifle, he poked the bears neck to be certain the animal was no longer a threat.

Exhaling the breath, he thought he'd held since he first saw his wife, he stretched to his full height and looked back at the trembling woman still seated beside the trail. He walked back to his wife and knelt in front of her, reached out to pull her to him and held her tight as she started to sob uncontrollably. Shortly she regained her composure and leaned back away from him and said, "You go get the horses!"

Talon chuckled at her remark and said, "How 'bout we go together?"

"Suits me, long as there ain't no more bears around. One's enough for me." She looked at the carcass in the trail and shook her head.

"Tell me about it," encouraged Talon.

She looked at her man and said, "I was just walkin' along mindin' my own business when he reared up in the trail and kinda tilted his head and growled at me. I think he was tryin' to tell me somethin' and Smokey was barkin' at him, but I just pulled the hammer back and shot at him from right here," she demonstrated her stance with the rifle held at her hip. "But I don't know if I hit him so I just kept shootin' an' shootin' I don't know how many times. I was too scared to count. When he finally fell down I shot him again an' he didn't move so I kinda fell down my own self and then you came along." She looked up at him and said, "What took you so long anyway?"

"Uh, uh, I came a runnin' after I heard the first shot… couldna been more a minute 'fore I got here. But it was all over but the shoutin'! You sure showed him who's boss of this trail." With his arm around her waist, he pulled her to him and gave her a sideways hug.

It was well after dark by the time they returned to camp with the carcass of the elk strapped to the mule's packs. Talon

43

said he'd retrieve the carcass of the bear after first light as Ginny cut a couple of elk steaks from the carcass and suspended them over the fire on fresh cut willow sticks. Both were hungry and tired and were looking forward to a good night's rest under the canopy of stars that strutted across the heavens along the milky way. It had been a good day.

Chapter Eight

LaPorte

THE BUCKBOARD WAS pulled by the mule that served Talon well as both a pack animal and to pull the wagon and maybe someday would be used to pull a plow. For now, they were only concerned with restocking their supplies at the general store in LaPorte. With the town being a primary re-supply stop for Oregon Trail bound wagon trains, the general store was larger and better stocked than most. But this late in the fall, wagon trains were non-existent and the general store was relatively empty of customers.

Talon tethered the mule to the rail in front of the store and walked with Ginny into the supply center of the town. A young man with curly brown hair stood behind the counter and held a newspaper in front of his face ignoring the couple as they browsed. Talon meandered to the counter and display of rifles and pistols and started naming off his needs for ammunition, powder, and lead. His Remington required powder and lead, while the Spencer and Henry used factory loaded cartridges. Ginny gave the young man her list of needs for the house and their supplies for the winter, beans, sugar, coffee, salt and many other items.

As he tallied up their bill and packaged their supplies, the young man looked at Ginny and asked, "Aren't you friends with Mary Sue Fredricks?"

"Why yes, I am, why do you ask?"

"Oh, you just looked familiar. I think I've seen you with Mary Sue a time or two," he said, apparently embarrassed.

"So, you know her well?"

"Not real well, but I've visited with her at Aunt Sophie's where she works. She sure is a fine young lady," he said as he busied himself with their supplies.

Ginny looked at the flustered young man and smiled to herself thinking of her friend and what she would say to her. They planned to go to Aunt Sophie's, the combination hotel and restaurant that was a staple of the town, and visit with Mary Sue and maybe see little Johnny as well. The three of them had been through a traumatic experience together when they were taken captive by the Cheyenne and Arapaho Dog Soldiers.

Talon had been the only one to come to their rescue and the four had become fast friends during the experience. Talon stood beside Ginny and settled their bill with the young man as he said, "By the way, my name is Grant Mullican, my father owns the store and if there's ever anything I can do for you, don't hesitate to ask."

"Thank you, Mr. Mullican, I'm Talon Thompsett and this is my wife, Virginia. We will keep that in mind and if we do need anything, we'll certainly come here."

They quickly loaded their supplies in the buckboard and Talon helped Ginny into the seat, untethered the mule and stepped up to the seat, took the reins and backed the mule away from the rail and started toward the hotel. Although Ginny and Mary Sue got together at every opportunity, those times were few and far between. Now Ginny was excited to see her lifelong friend again and was thinking about what might be going on between her and Grant Mullican.

As they walked through the door, Mary Sue immediately spotted the duo and ran toward them with arms stretched wide and a smile splitting her face. "Ginny! Talon! It's so good to see you two, it seems like forever since we saw each other," she said as she gave Ginny a big hug and smiled at Talon.

"Where's that little Johnny? I hoped to see him this time around," asked Talon.

"He's at school, silly. Don't you know that boys his age are supposed to be in school?" replied Mary Sue as she escorted them to a table.

"Well, I guess I plum forgot."

"It sure is good to see the two of you," said Mary Sue reaching out to take Ginny's hand.

"You said that already," replied Ginny, "So, how is everything? Have you met anyone new?" Ginny smiled as she waited for Mary Sue to tell her about Grant Mullican.

"Oh, just the usual folks around town and an occasional traveler, you know how it is. This time of year, most folks are getting ready for winter and don't have much time for coming to town," answered Mary Sue.

"Well, we met someone that seems to be taken with you!" The two women leaned toward one another in a conspiratorial manner. Talon just shook his head and grinned. It was good to see the two friends enjoying their time together, even if they were plotting someone's capture in the web of love.

With lunch finished and Mary Sue's needing to get back to work, the friends said their goodbyes and Talon and Ginny stepped outside to be greeted by the bright sun that hung suspended directly overhead. The arching blue sky was a welcome sight and the few trees around town were showing their fall colors or losing their foliage in anticipation of the colder months ahead.

Ginny said, "I just remembered, I was gonna stop at the millinery and talk to Gertrude about a pattern. I'll just be a minute," as she started down the boardwalk toward the women's shop. Talon untied the mule and backed the wagon away from the rail, turned the wagon around and slapped the mule's backside with the reins to pull to the front of the millinery.

Talon's attention was suddenly taken by a ruckus across the street in front of the general store. He stepped from the wagon and started in that direction. Randall Jackson, a farmer from north of town was using a bullwhip on his field hand , a big nigra that was bent over at the waist and taking the beating across his back.

Talon trotted over to the boardwalk where several people watched the whipping. When the whip snaked back for another strike, Talon caught the tip and wrapped the slack around his wrist. As Jackson started to flay the back of the big man with another strike, he brought his arm forward and was suddenly stopped as Talon jerked back on the whip.

Jackson lost his balance, stumbled sideways and turned with a snarl on his face. He was a big man; close to six feet and broad as a single tree across the shoulders with a thick chest that showed through his loose linsey Woolsey shirt. Galuses held up woolen trousers that hung high above his ankles giving the impression he was holding them up to cross a stream.

He jerked on his whip but Talon held it fast. Jackson snarled through tobacco stained teeth, "You better let that go, sonny, or I'll take it to your backside."

Talon looked at the braided leather whip's end in his hand and back at Jackson and said, "Oh, you mean this?" motioning to the whip. "Why, I was just gonna show you how to use it proper."

"Whaddayou mean? Show me how to use it?" said the big man, looking down at the whip's handle now held loosely in his open palm.

"Why, you weren't accomplishin' nuthin' the way you were handlin' it. Let me show you how to do real damage," and with a sudden jerk he snatched the whip from the big man's grasp.

He stood with a smile on his face as he coiled the whip at his side, then motioned to the folks behind him to move and let the coils smoothly snake out with his arm outstretched away from the crowd. He grinned at the big man, looked at the nigra that now stood facing him, and quickly brought the full length of the whip in a sidearm motion and without striking anything, let the whip crack in the air with the sound of a rifle shot.

Every one of the spectators jumped slightly at the loud report and they watched as Talon brought it back for another strike. Without hesitation, he brought it forward again and cracked it just over the top of Jackson's head, causing the man to reach up to protect his face and tuck his head and neck into his shoulders.

The alarm on the big man's face turned to fury and he started toward Talon only to be stopped by another crack of the whip that cut one of the galuses on his britches making him stop in his tracks. He grabbed at that side of his britches only to have the other strap of his galuses cut by Talon's next whip crack.

The big bully stood with two hands holding up his britches and a snarl on his face that would have wilted a lesser man than Talon.

"Now sir, let me explain something. This is Colorado Territory and we are under territorial law, which means slavery is outlawed. So, any hold you have on that man," motioning to the big black man that now stood tall but with a bewildered expression on his face, "does not allow you to whip him. But just so you'll understand the way folks hereabouts think about those things, let me give you a reminder of the perils of whipping."

In a surprising move, Talon again snaked the whip forward and cut the man's shirt, bringing blood to a thin line across his chest. The bully looked at his chest and absent mindedly let go of his britches to pull his shirt together causing his britches to sag to his knees revealing his faded red union suit. He reached down to pull at his britches and looked in fear toward Talon, expecting another strike of the whip.

Talon stood with a somber expression as he watched the embarrassment of the big man and slowly coiled the whip. He said, "I think I'll just drop this off at the constable's office because I don't think you're going to be needing it anytime soon. You probably oughta get you some new duds, don'tcha think?"

The gathered crowd laughed and broke out into applause as Talon turned away and started for the office of the local law. The bully knew he had no recourse, not with the whole town on Talon's side. Talon motioned to the black man to join him and the confused former slave trotted after the tall young man.

As the man caught up to him, Talon asked, "What's your name?"

"Uh, muh name's Moses, but most folks just call me Mose."

The two men walked side by side down the boardwalk as Talon asked, "Were you that man's slave?"

"He says I is, but I won my freedom aftuh servin' with the Army."

Talon stopped and looked at the man and said, "Well, how did you come to get hooked up with that man?"

"Uh, I stopped at his place lookin' fo' work, and he put me to work clearin' his fields. But aftuh I worked a few days and et his grub, he said I owed him and that made me his slave."

"Was that the first time he whipped you?" asked Talon.

"Nosuh, he done that most ever' day," replied Mose with his head hanging down.

"Well, Mose, you are not anyone's slave. You heard me tell that man about the law of the territory and with your time in the army, you are definitely a free man. I'll tell you what, I'll talk to the station keeper at the Overland line and we'll see about gettin' you a job and a place to stay. Would that be alright with you?"

Mose let a big grin spread across his midnight black face and said, "Yessuh, yessuh, that'd be mighty fine, suh."

"And I ain't no sir, I'm just Talon," assured the young man. He knew Mose had to be close to twice his age and he certainly didn't want any man calling him sir.

After explaining the situation to the constable, Talon was assured by him that the law was on his side. He left the whip with the authorities and walked with Mose to the stage station. When he explained the circumstances, the keeper said if Talon was willing to take him on the next run, the station at Bijou Creek needed help but the man could work at LaPorte until that time.

As he started to leave, Mose asked, "Would it be ahright if I brought my wife along too?" Both Talon and the station keeper looked at him then exchanged glances before the keeper said, "I do believe havin' your wife along would be a good thing. Can she cook?"

"Oh yessuh, my wife's the best cook aroun'! She can make anything taste mighty fine," he said grinning at the thought of the many meals made from simple things but became fit for a king.

Talon looked at the station keeper and said, "Well, I'll let you take it from here. I've got to get back to my wife before she buys out the whole town!"

Both men laughed as the tall young man left the station in search of his wife.

To The Overland Trail

Chapter Nine

Preparations

WINTER IN THE MOUNTAINS is not to be entered into unprepared. If the mountains could talk they would tell the tales of many presumptuous explorers that dared to compare the high-altitude winters to those of the lowlands. Having never experienced the brittle temperatures of the deep of winter that caused even the pines to groan in agony, many were the fools that thought they could endure and became nothing more than a carcass for the carrion-eaters like the coyote, vultures, eagles and others.

Talon was no stranger to the perils of mountain winters that went from blue sky and sunshine to raging blizzards in a matter of hours. He knew it would take more than a cozy cabin to survive and he set about to ensure his new wife would not want for anything during the times his job at the stage line took him away from home.

Sitting at the table and enjoying his morning coffee, he began to share with Ginny about the preparations that needed to be completed. "We're gonna need a root cellar to keep our meat and other supplies and it'll need to be strong and secure 'cause there's always some bears that are late gettin' to their dens to hibernate and will try to get anything they can to finish out their fat."

"Well, will that elk and the bear we already got be enough to last?"

"No, and that also means we'll have to do some more huntin'," answered Talon.

"And what else will we need to do?" asked a concerned Ginny as she reached across the table to take Talon's hand.

"Well, I'll need to lay in a good supply of firewood, at least a couple o' cords, probably more. Then we need to take stock of our other supplies and make another trip into town to finish out our stock," he said as he looked at his coffee before taking another sip as he tried to think of all that needed to be done. He reflected on the winters at the ranch and the many preparations his family undertook to make for a comfortable winter, and pictured the home place and his family and got a glassy-eyed stare as he reminisced. Ginny looked at him and wondered aloud, "Now where did you just go? You looked like you were a million miles away."

"Nah, I was just rememberin' all the things my family would do before winter set in just so's I'd not forget anything," he grinned and squeezed her hand.

"I sure don't like leavin' you here by yourself, course you are an ol' bear killer so I s'pose you'll be alright," he mused as he looked at her with a touch of mischief in his eyes.
Ginny playfully slapped him on the shoulder and said, "You better believe it buster, ain't nothin' gonna happen that I can't take care of, me an' my Henry over there," as she motioned to the rifle standing beside the door.

"Well, c'mon then, we'll take the wagon up the trail aways and get some o' them lodgepole pine to line the root cellar. It'll be a lot easier haulin' 'em in the wagon instead of snakin' 'em outta the timber," he instructed as he rose from the chair and headed for the door, grabbing his hat from the peg by the entry and lookin' back at Ginny as she snatched her jacket off the back of the chair.

The day was spent with Talon swinging the double-bladed axe to cut the slender and straight lodgepole pine while Ginny used the hatchet to de-limb each pole. By the end of the day, both were rubbing their shoulders and upper arms from the soreness but they were happy with the big load on the wagon. The next two days were spent digging out the root cellar that was only a couple of yards to the side of the cabin.

The following day saw the finishing of the cellar with lodgepoles lining the walls, ceiling and even the floor, with several cut short to make the stairs leading down into the cellar. The roof was heaped over with the dug-out soil and all was complete with a split-log door that secured the entryway.

Three more days were spent felling the standing dead pines nearby and splitting the wood for use in the stove. The firewood was stacked alongside the cabin to make it easy to get to on those cold winter days. The two stood back from the cabin and surveyed their handiwork and hugged each other with tired arms and sore muscles but satisfied spirits. This would be their first winter together and they both knew they were making special memories.

"Well, I guess we better take stock of our supplies and make that trip into town you talked about. I tell you what, let's make us a list so we'll be sure to get everything. Oh, and by the way, Mary Sue told me about a farmer woman that had put up a bunch of canned goods and she would be willin' to do some tradin' or outright sell 'em. You think we could stop by her place and see what she has?" asked Ginny as the two walked toward the cabin with arms loosely around each other's waists and Smokey leading the way to their home.

"Of course, that'll be fine, an' what she doesn't have we can get at the store. And before you even ask, yes, we'll stop and see Mary Sue," replied Talon grinning.

The short ride to town was a pleasant one as they looked at the remnants of color on the cottonwoods and the few patches of aspen that crawled up the ridges on the South side of the river. Ginny giggled as she watched a squirrel with his cheeks stuffed with nuts scampering up a tree to his secret hidey-hole. A big jack rabbit hopped across the road in front of them only to disappear beneath a patch of buffalo-berry bushes between the road and the river.

As they neared the town, Ginny said, "Drop me off at Gertie's, she should have that pattern for me by now. I'll meet you over at the general store in just a couple of minutes."

"Okay then, but don't be too long 'cause I'm gettin' hungry and I'm lookin' forward to lunch at Aunt Sophie's."

"What, isn't my cooking good enough for you?" asked Ginny appearing to pout in disappointment.

"Of course, your cookin's fine, I'm just hungry that's all," explained Talon.

She playfully slapped his arm again and said, "That better be all there is to that, because if not, you'll hurt my feelings. And when my feelings are hurt, I just can't find my way to the kitchen."

"Alright, alright, I get the message. Here's Gertie's, and I'll be waitin' at the store."

As Ginny and Smokey disappeared into the millinery, Talon steered the mule to the general store and stepped down to tether the mule before starting for the store. He was lost in thought, thinking about the way Ginny had kidded him and the work they had done together. It had been a good week and more and he was feeling much better about the coming winter.

As he took a step up to the boardwalk, he was suddenly struck by the crack of a bullwhip across his back. He fell forward and rolled over and caught another strike on his shoulder. As the whip lacerated his jacket, he reached out trying to grab the lash before it was drawn back but all his hand caught was air.

Again, the braided leather whispered through the air seeking its target. Talon dropped his head behind his uplifted arm and struggled to his feet as the popper wrapped around his arm and was pulled back. Before the whip could be retrieved, Talon had a grasp of the fall, the section of the whip behind the popper and tied to the thong or long braided stretch of the whip. But the strength of Randall Jackson ripped it from his hand and snaked it back for another strike as the big man snarled, "Now, I'll show you how to use a whip you little pup! You robbed me of my slave and now you're gonna pay!"

The whip streaked out but Talon dropped to the ground and the popper snapped in the air with a loud crack. Jackson quickly retrieved it and started to strike again but Talon dropped his shoulder and bulled into the chest of the big man, startling him and driving him back against the rail beside the water trough. He tried to push Talon off but was met with the hard knuckles of Talon as they crashed into his broad and now flattened nose.

He screamed as blood spurted all over his face and he forced himself off the rail as he pushed against his much younger adversary. Talon stepped back and through slit eyes he watched as the bully tried to retrieve his whip, but before he could bring his arm forward, Talon drove in with both arms pumping as he pounded the midriff of the big man who gasped for air.

Jackson dropped the whip and wrapped his arms around Talon, pinning his arms to his sides. Through his brown teeth he growled, "Now I'm gonna take pleasure in squeezing the life right outta you, you young whippersnapper."

His foul breath did as much damage as his grip and Talon knew he would hear ribs break if he didn't get out of this man's grasp. He reared his head back and with all the force he could muster, he snapped his head forward and flattened the bloody pulp of Jackson's nose across his face. The big man screamed and released Talon so he could grab at his own face as if feeling his nose would make it better. Talon immediately loosed a flurry of blows to Jackson's middle and heard ribs break as the big man sunk to his knees.

He reached for Talon, but the young man sidestepped his reach. Grabbing the rail behind him, Jackson struggled to his feet, hanging his head and holding his face. He mumbled something and turned to face Talon.

Talon watched but did not attack. Jackson shook his head side to side and looked like a grizzly bear as he plodded toward Talon, growling with every step. He surprised Talon with a back hand that sent him stumbling and the big man surprised the watching crowd as he leaped to grab at Talon's jacket and turn him around to face a massive fist that came flying toward his face. Talon turned and took the blow to the side of the head that caused him to see stars and stagger to the side as darkness threatened to overtake him, but he knew if he fell the big man would beat him to death.

Talon stepped away from the monster and drew a deep breath then surprised the big man as he stepped toward him. The bully fully expected the younger man to turn and try to flee and he wasn't expecting an attack, but attack Talon did, bringing his next blow from beside his foot and brought it up to meet the big man's chin, snapping his head back.

Jackson staggered but Talon continued his onslaught with a roundhouse left that caught Jackson on the side of his face, whipping his head around and bringing a cloud of blackness across his eyes. When he began to fall, Talon grabbed his shirt and pulled him back with his left hand and delivered another fist to his face with his right. He released his grip and let the big man fall. He watched as Jackson rolled to one side and with his free arm, he waved his open hand as if he were surrendering and calling an end to the scrap.

Talon stood bent over with hands on his knees and sucking for air as he watched Jackson crawl toward the water trough. He turned his back on the bully and started for his wagon in front of the general store when someone shouted, "Look Out!"

Suddenly a rifle barked and several in the crowd gasped. Talon whirled to see Jackson with his rifle half out of the scabbard under his saddle on the tall black horse tethered to the rail.

His eyes were big and an expression of fear painted his face as he looked across the street to see a smoking Henry cradled in the Ginny's arms.

Jackson looked at the rail beside him and saw the furrow made by the slug from the Henry and he looked back again at the woman holding the rifle. He slid his rifle back in the scabbard and slowly mounted his horse to leave. He looked at the many faces of the crowd on the boardwalk and realized that everyone that had once been a friend, now saw him for what he was, a bully and a coward who had been beaten by a man half his age. He knew he was no longer welcome and he reined his horse toward the road out of town.

Talon looked at Ginny and said, "You're pretty handy to have around."

"If you're just now realizing that, we need to talk," replied the woman with a gun.

Talon nodded his head and replied, "Yes, m'am."

To The Overland Trail

Chapter Ten

Retaliation

SEVERAL DOG SOLDIER bands continued their resistance to the treaties between the whites and the Cheyenne and Arapaho. After Black Kettle and White Antelope led their villages to Fort Lyon and accepted the blue coats offer of peace and safety, many of the leaders and bands of both the Cheyenne and Arapaho refused to follow Black Kettle and split off and formed their own villages and bands. The Dog Soldiers continued their attacks on the wagon trains, ranches, small villages and stage stations and now many others stood with them and their attempts to drive the whites from their lands.

The blue coats retaliated with assaults on villages suspected of involvement with those attacks. Spotted Crow of the Cheyenne and Heap of Buffalo and Neva of the Arapaho had joined their forces of warriors and now presented the largest contingent of Dog Soldier supporters. With warriors of the Lakota joining them, the Dog Soldiers were increasing the number of attacks on the whites and often returned to this village to recoup.

The great warrior of the Cheyenne, Roman Nose, walked with Black Wolf and Red Hawk of the Dog Soldiers and spoke, "You make war on the whites, but what have you accomplished?"

The excited Red Hawk quickly responded, "We have captured many horses, taken many scalps and stolen many weapons!"

"Yes, but have the whites left the land?"

"No, but their spirits have. When they are killed like the dogs they are, the others see what waits for them and we have seen some going back to the place of the rising sun," answered Black Wolf.

"I believe what you have done is anger the whites even more. They will have their blue coats continue to attack our villages and kill our women and children and old men," somberly stated Roman Nose. "I am a warrior and I want to see the blood of many whites on my knife and their scalps on my lance, but I want to see the people come together and wipe the whites from the land. What you do with your raids does not do this. You kill a few and take their horses and weapons, but more come and soon there will be even more blue coats."

"Would you have us wait? And for what and for how long? I see our leaders begging for peace and crawling to the blue coats on their bellies like the snakes they have become. They will not gather our peoples together to fight, but to crawl like cowards into some corner and die," vehemently spat Black Wolf. "You are a great warrior, Roman Nose, you must join us!"

The respected warrior stopped and turned to the younger men, placed his hand on Black Wolf's shoulder and said, "I will not join you now. I will wait to see what our leaders do and then decide. You and your warriors must continue to fight until that time."

Black Wolf and Red Hawk looked at one another and shouted "Aiiiieeee" in response to this encouragement from the great Roman Nose. They watched as he returned to his lodge. Black Wolf looked at Red Hawk and said, "You go and get Walks with Bear, Little Paw and Raven. Bring them to my lodge, we must plan our next attacks on the whites!"

When the other Dog Soldier leaders joined him, Black Wolf started their council of war with the pipe. After the somber passing and smoking of the pipe, Black Wolf began, "We have done well with our attacks on the whites, but we must continue and do even more!"

The others nodded their heads and muttered their agreement. Raven spoke up, "We have had many warriors join us and we can take more scalps from the whites, but with the winter storms coming, it will be hard."

Again, the heads nodded and mumbled remarks made to one another. "If we strike soon, we can take more horses and our village can move easier with more horses. That will keep the blue coats from finding us," said Walks with Bear.

"The coming of winter will also make the whites think they are safe and we will surprise them and have an easy victory!" declared Little Paw. His remark drew many nods of acceptance and remarks of agreement.

Black Wolf grinned at the positive response of the warriors and said, "We do have many more warriors and I believe we should attack many places to confuse the whites. I will lead my band to take the stage stations beyond the grass land and the flat top mountain. Little Paw will take his band against the stations to the North that are near the river the whites call South Platte. Walks with Bear, you will attack the ranches and others that are along the river to the South of us. Raven will join Little Paw and Red Hawk will come with me."

The men looked from one to another, nodding their heads in agreement and anticipation of the coming battles. Raven said, "Black Wolf has chosen wisely. We will make war against the whites and soon they will leave our land!"

The others shouted their agreement and stood to leave and prepare for their attacks. Black Wolf's band would have to travel the furthest, a distance of three to four days, before they could mount their assault. But he felt his attack would be the most effective for the whites would believe there was no place that would be safe from their attacks and the plunder from the stage stations always yielded weapons and many horses. He was anxious for another battle and quickly began to prepare by packing his parfleche with smoked meat, pemmican, dried berries and more.

He had a Hawken rifle and would need extra powder and lead which he also put in the parfleche. He selected a coat stolen when they raided a ranch, a blanket coat made from a wool Hudson Bay blanket. When he wore the striped coat, he was easily visible and he liked the idea of his enemies knowing he was attacking. He thought the coat gave him power and he liked its warmth in these colder days.

November in Colorado territory ushered in the blistering cold of winter. The low rolling hills of the Eastern plains offered little protection and the few buttes with their escarpments of granite served both animal and man when the winter storms whistled through the flats. The howling winds turned the storm into a merciless rage that used the icy snow to cut any exposed flesh and deliver its painful frost bite.

The twelve warriors that followed Black Wolf were wrapped in blankets and buffalo robes with their faces buried deep and allowed their horses to blindly follow the deep red patches of color on their leader's mount. The sudden storm struck with ferocity while they made their way across the flats and now they struggled to find the distant butte for some semblance of protection.

Black Wolf's horse stumbled but continued at the urging of his rider. Whenever there was a break in the wind, Black Wolf corrected the direction that led them into the face of the storm, but closer to the butte. When they finally reached the lee side of the flat top, a thick cluster of juniper and pinion trees beckoned and the war party quickly huddled together within the copse of trees.

A few of the men gathered branches of grey dead wood to start a fire while others made fast the horses. Within moments, there was a fire blazing in the small clearing protected by the towering butte and the thick grove of trees. The men gathered around the fire, stretched out stiff fingers and sought the warmth the blaze offered. There was no conversation as each man thought of the warm lodges they left behind. Would this be worth the sacrifice?

To The Overland Trail

Chapter Eleven

Shotgun

"WE'RE CARRYIN' SOME purty important people this time aroun'," drawled Bull as he slapped the lines on the rumps of the horses to start them off from the North Platte station. They were on the flip side of their round-about from LaPorte. Two days travel were made in peace as they came from LaPorte to North Platte and they were now headed to their home station.

Talon's reputation of attracting Indian attacks had taken a hit with the entire trip being made without sighting one single Indian. The previous driver that was teamed with Talon, Mac MacGillicutty, had often kidded Talon that the only time he experienced an attack by Indians was when Talon was aboard.

That reputation had followed Talon during his short time as a Shotgun with the Overland Stage line and Bull poked him in the ribs when he added, "And since we got those bigshots travelin' with us you better hope your Indian magnet ain'ta workin'. That's all we need is to have to fight off some Cheyenne just to save the skin of them city slickers back there."

"Just who are they anyway?" asked Talon.

"Wal, one of 'ems the division agent for the stage line. He's s'posed to be in charge of everythin' from Denver to Salt Lake. An' the other'n is some bigshot with Western Union, the telegraph comp'ny. Way I hear it is Western Union is wantin' to take over every'thin' from the American Telegraph comp'ny. I guess he's checkin' all the home stations an' their telegraph set-ups."

"An' who's the married couple?" inquired Talon.

"Dunno, I think he's s'posed to be some kinda politician, but other'n that, I dunno," answered Bull as he see-sawed the lines to guide the leaders on the roadway.

"Well, I guess we got our work cut out for us, babysittin' this bunch. Reckon I better keep the Indians at least arm-distance away, ya think?"

Bull chuckled at the image of allowing a rampaging Indian even that close and shook his head at his young partner. He hoped the return trip was just as boring as the trip out. The only breaks in the monotony of the familiar route was the passing of the traveling blacksmithy and harness maker who normally traveled this route with his specially fitted wagon complete with bellows and tools for tending the many horses used by the stage line.

It was at the Little Laramie swing station at the crossing of the Laramie river they passed the blacksmith. It was right after they passed the two freight wagons, each pulled by a six-up of mules, that were carrying supplies to each of the stage stations along the line. If everything went right on this trip, they would be sleeping at Big Laramie tonight and be home to LaPorte by the following night.

Their first change of horses came at Pass Creek and was quickly accomplished. Bull wanted to get through Rattlesnake Canyon with the full light of morning. The canyon seemed to be a favorite place for Indian attacks and he wanted it behind him as soon as possible. With an easy pass through the dreaded canyon, the next stop was Whiskey Gap and Fort Halleck. A simple meal of bacon, biscuits and coffee let them get on their way without loss of time. None of the stations reported any sign of Indians and Bull was getting hopeful for a nice quiet trip.

Elk Mountain provided a quick change of horses and they were soon on the part of the road that turned toward the South. With the sun coming onto his right shoulder, Bull began to relax and let the horses have their heads and the pace increased just a bit. Winter had been slow in coming to the East West stretch from the Laramie River to the Green Rivers, but whenever it was slow in coming, it usually made up for it with greater snow depth and a much longer season. The wind became cold and both men wrapped themselves in their buffalo robes, turning up the big collars to shield their necks and pulling the felt hats down to shield their faces.

They could see the makings of a storm to the South East and they were hopeful they would beat the storm to Big Laramie station so they could have warm accommodations for the night. The horses were feeling the cold as they dropped their heads and slowed their pace. Bull shouted, "Ándele" to encourage the horses to keep their pace.

Rock Creek provided a short break for the crew and passengers alike to warm up by the stove and for the hostler to change the teams, but Bull was anxious to get moving and hopefully beat the storm to Big Laramie.

"Alright folks, we need to get a move on, so get aboard so we can make time," he ordered. Although they grumbled about leaving the warmth of the stove and station, they knew the Jehu was right and quickly boarded. Talon stood the Henry between his knees and pulled down his hat, turned up his collar, and put his hands in opposite sleeves like a big muff. Hunkering down he mumbled to Bull, "Hey, you big Ox, try to find a route around this cold wind, will'ya'?"

"Boy, you know I would if I could," replied the big man as he grabbed the lines and slapped the horses into action. Because of the need of holding the lines separate through his fingers, Bull's meaty paws didn't allow for gloves and he had to suffer the cold wind continually assaulting his hands. His fingers and palms were calloused and cracked with the chafing of the leather, but the big man acted like it was nothing and continued handling the reins like they were warm ribbons on a Christmas package.

Talon peered out from his self-induced hideaway to survey the surrounding countryside. The thick dark storm clouds gave the appearance of dusk and limited his view, but he felt the weather favored their safety because the Indians didn't like the cold any more than he did. Yet he continually watched.

The hostler at Rock Creek told them the news of an Indian attack at the Fletcher ranch out on the flats and the killing of the mother and the wounding of the father and brother. They also abducted the two girls, Mary, 13, and Lizzie, 2. The news of the recent attack made Talon even more vigilant, yet as he watched he remembered.

It hadn't been that long ago when he gave the Cheyenne chase when they stole two young women and a boy. He had been successful in their rescue and married one of the women, Ginny. But he knew what the younger girls would be faced with and he knew there was very little hope for their return.

Nearing the next swing station, Cooper Creek, the stage topped a small rise that provided a view of the location of the station. They were greeted by the smell of smoke as the cold wind drove the cloud toward the stage. Bull leaned back with a firm grip on the lines as he stood slightly and looked at the scene a short distance away. Blackened timbers were all that remained of the station and barn, but off to the side lay an overturned freight wagon and behind it the charred remains of another.

Talon stretched up and pushed his hat back as he looked at the destruction before him. He quickly looked around for any sign of the attackers, but the only movement was the cold wind blowing smoke and ashes.

Bull slapped the horses to move forward slowly. As they drew nearer they spotted bodies; first the teamsters by the freight wagons, bloody, mutilated and scalped bodies. The carcasses of the mules were still in their harnesses, slaughtered and left for scavengers, most Indians had no use for the draft type animals. The station keeper and the hostler, or what was left of them, were propped against the half-burned logs of the station. The stench of burnt flesh prompted both Bull and Talon to duck their heads below their collars. Beyond the station were the remains of the blacksmith wagon, also burnt, and the smithy's body partially obscured by the remains.

Both Bull and Talon knew they couldn't take the time to bury the bodies. If they remained here any longer they would endanger their passengers, the cargo and themselves. With the impending storm, they had to push on. Although the distance to Little Laramie was less than 10 miles, their stop for the night was to be Big Laramie, which was almost 20 miles away. They were hopeful Little Laramie would be intact and able to provide a relief team, but now they would have to take this team double the usual distance.

Talon leaned over to tell the passengers, "Folks, you prob'ly saw the station an' such, but we can't stop. We'll have to take it easy till we get to the next station, horses are tired, but there's the danger of Indians. So, if you folks're armed, it might be a good idea to stay watchful. Them Indians are prob'ly long gone and we should be safe enough, but consider yourselves warned."

He heard some grumbling from inside the coach but couldn't make out what was being said and didn't really care, for there was nothing anyone could do about the situation but ride it out.

Bull let the horses walk for a while and then kicked them up to a canter for a couple of miles and let them walk for a few more. By alternating their pace, he knew they should be able to make the distance but just take a little longer.

Late afternoon brought a lull in the wind and the sight of Little Laramie, still standing. When the keeper and hostler were informed about the fate of Cooper Creek, they hastened the harnessing of the new team and sent the stage on its way. With only two men manning this swing station, they knew they were in danger of an attack and they wanted to fortify the place as much as possible. Before the stage pulled away, they retreated into the log station building and started shuttering the windows.

Bull shook his head as they left and said just loud enough for Talon to hear, "I shore don't envy them boys, nossiree."

Talon nodded his head in agreement.

They arrived at Big Laramie just as the sun tucked itself behind the distant Elk Mountain and were happy to turn the stage and team over to the hostler and his helpers. With Big Laramie a home station, they had a telegraph and the word was quickly sent to the other locations with a telegrapher about the attack on Cooper Creek.

Cooper Creek station destroyed by Indians. 5 killed. Nearby ranch also attacked, 1 killed, two wounded, 2 children taken.

They knew the word would be spread even further and Talon was concerned about his wife learning of the attack and that she would be worried about him, but he was hopeful she would be still at home at the cabin and wouldn't come to town until he was due to return the next night, at least that was the plan.

Chapter Twelve

Chivington

THE OFFICE WAS PANELED with imported black walnut and bookcases covered the entire west wall. Every shelf was stuffed with leather bound and gold inscribed books that were impressive for their appearance as well as titles. Brocade drapes hung loosely to the sides of the two windows that were the sole source of light.

The morning sun illuminated the massive oak desk that partially obscured the tall black leather tufted chair that held John Evans, the governor of Colorado Territory. He leaned back in his throne-like chair and absentmindedly twisted the end of his moustache between his fingers. Looking at the man across the desk, he said, "John, these continued reports of Indian attacks on our stage stations and settlers is not what I expected when I appointed you Colonel of the 1st Colorado Cavalry. After that Hungate massacre, with the whole family killed and especially those two little girls, I thought the citizenry would be mad enough to do something, but even your Captain Davidson couldn't accomplish his task of getting the Arapahos that did it. Why, there's even some of the bleedin' hearts from back East that are sympathizin' with those red-skinned murders."

He paused and took a deep breath to settle himself and began again, "Now, John, we've been friends a long time and we've accomplished a lot together. Why, just yesterday the chancellor of Colorado Seminary told me how well the school is doing." Leaning forward, he pointed his finger at Chivington and continued, "the school you and I founded, and how pleased he is with their progress. Our territory is growing and even after the gold is playing out in South Park, the influx of settlers has not waned. But these attacks have got to stop! When word gets around that we haven't settled the Indian problem, both our careers will be over. Now, I know you aspire to a career in politics, and this kind of failure will doom you before you even start."

The governor leaned back in his chair to give the Reverend Colonel John Chivington time to decide on a course of action. He was startled by the vehemence of his reply, "Damn any man who sympathizes with Indians! I have come to kill Indians, and believe it is right and honorable to use any means under God's heaven to kill Indians. Kill and scalp them all, big and little; nits make lice!" He slapped his palm down on the arm of his chair to emphasize his point.

Evans jerked slightly at the sound but let a grin cross his face. "That's more like it. Now, after these recent attacks, the people are angered and they want to see the Indians gone. They won't put up with these attacks without some kind of action taken to teach them cursed animals a lesson they won't soon forget. When I issued the proclamation last August that authorized citizens to go in pursuit of all hostiles and kill and destroy the enemies of Colorado, I really thought more of our citizens would act upon that. But that has proven me wrong, and now we've got to do something. Any ideas?"

"Well, John," started Chivington as he leaned forward, placing his forearms on the edge of the desk, "After I complained to Curtis about that Indian lover, Major Wynkoop, he finally agreed to replace him. His successor, Major Anthony, agrees with us about the need to eradicate the Indians. Curtis also agreed to stop the protection and provisioning of those Arapaho and Cheyenne camped out there beyond Fort Lyon, and if that doesn't drive them out, I'm sure if we combine the 1st Colorado with the 3rd Colorado Cavalry, we can convince them to leave this territory." He leaned back in his chair with a smug look on his face as if he had handed the governor the solution to his Indian dilemma.

The governor stared at the man before him and considered not just what he said, but what was implied. He looked down at his folded hands that rested on the surface of the desk and his shoulders slumped a bit before he pushed himself up and turned to look at the large territorial map that hung on the wall behind his desk.

He motioned for Chivington to join him. Placing the flat of his palm on the Northwest quadrant of the map he started, "John, the most recent attacks have been north of here at these stage stations," pointing at the Overland Stage line route that went from LaPorte to Virginia Dale, "and those attacks weren't even in Colorado territory!

But I just got word of more attacks over here..." He pointed at the Overland Trail that led to Julesburg. "You and your Lieutenant, what's his name, have hit the Indian villages here," pointing to an area North East of the territorial boundary, "and here," pointing to the Southeast quadrant of the map. "It seems to have been nothing more than a game of tic-tac-toe between you and the Cheyenne. So, whatever we do next has got to be decisive and send a very strong message!" He pounded one fist into the palm of the other hand.

Turning back to his desk and reseating himself, he watched as the contemplative Chivington walked to his chair, one hand behind his back and the other stroking his beard. "Governor, I believe the greatest concentration of Cheyenne and Arapaho is out beyond Fort Lyon. If I take my troops down there, I believe we can surprise them and have a decisive victory that will eliminate most of the Indians and strike fear in the hearts of any others. When they know that Colorado won't tolerate their actions or even their presence, they will be gone!"

Governor Evans looked at his friend and contemplated what he was suggesting. He knew Chivington felt exactly like he did... that Indians needed to be totally eradicated. Why, their very presence stifled his plans for a greater Colorado and a greater position of influence for himself. A slow grin started as he nodded his head, "And I think I can give you an additional company of troops. The 1st New Mexico Volunteers are looking for something to do to get involved and this is just the thing. But John, if you do this, it best be a complete eradication or the others will come back to haunt the both of us. Do I make myself clear?"

Chivington quickly stood, stretched out his hand and said, "Completely, John, completely!"

The two men shook hands and Chivington departed with an anxious grin crossing his face. This was just exactly what he wanted, and more. With the attachment of the New Mexico volunteers, his troop would number almost 800. More than enough to take on the entire Cheyenne and Arapaho nation.

As his pace increased, he began mentally calculating the supplies and weaponry he would need for his eradication campaign. He slapped his gloves on the side of his leg and barely stifled a shout of exultation as he contemplated the fulfillment of his campaign dreams.

For many years while he served as a Methodist minister in Illinois, Nebraska and finally Colorado, he thought his calling as minister would be his ultimate glory. But when the Civil War broke out and the then Governor Gilpin offered him a commission as a chaplain, he refused it, saying he wanted to fight.

However, the grandeur he sought was elusive but now he would have that honor that had escaped him when he was at the Glorieta Pass engagement. The glory he longed for and believed he deserved. This would be his launch up the political ladder and the greatness he believed was his destiny.

To The Overland Trail

Chapter Thirteen

Carson

TALON STEPPED INTO the stage station at LaPorte to check on his next scheduled run. When he noticed the station keeper busy with a man leaning on the counter, Talon stepped to the side and waited for the conversation to ebb. He casually looked at the man, apparently someone booking passage to Golden City, and noticed his buckskin attire. His trousers were cut and trimmed in the usual fashion of an Indian, but his coat, though buckskin was lined with what appeared to be the fur of a wolf. With his coat hanging open, his buckskin shirt showed elaborate bead work and elk's tooth decorations, the kind of work only done by a skillful Indian, maybe Cheyenne, for they were noted for their exquisite beadwork.

The station keeper, Henry Porter, apparently finished with his ticketing, motioned for Talon to step forward as he said, "Thompsett, I want you to meet this fella, he'll be travelin' on the next stage out goin' East. Mr. Carson, this is one of our Shotgunners, Talon Thompsett. Talon, this is Mr. Kit Carson."

"Whoa now, easy on the Mr., I'm just Kit," he said to Henry Porter and turned to shake Talon's outstretched hand.

"Thompsett ya say? I knowed a Thompsett onct, up in the Wind Rivers, he any kin of yourn?" drawled the man. He was leaning against the counter and it was difficult to discern his height, but it was evident he had to look up at Talon. Carson was a well-built man with a deep chest, long blonde hair that hung to his shoulders and a clean-shaven face. His deep set blue eyes were friendly but alert to everything around him. He lifted his eyebrows as he looked at Talon and waited for his answer.

Talon was surprised to meet this man whose reputation was twice as big as he was, a well-known mountain man that rode with Jim Bridger and a scout and guide for John Fremont. Talon stuttered a mite as he responded, "Uh, uh, yessir, if you're talkin' about Jeremiah Thompsett, he lived, well still does live, in the Wind Rivers with his family and the Arapaho. He's my grandfather."

"Well, I'll be hornswaggled! If'n that don't beat all, ol' Jeremiah havin' grandkids. I'da never imagined it. Why boy, yore granddaddy an me spent some shinin' times with them 'rapahos, yessir, we did. Why my wife an . . .who'd he take for his woman anyway?" asked the mountain man.

"He married Laughing Waters, her brother, Broken Shield is the chief of that band and she's the Shaman," declared Talon.

Carson slapped his knee and cackled and looked up at the young man before him and said, "Why, my first wife, Waanibe, or Singing Grass, and your Grandma was best friends. Well, well, if that don't beat all. And I thought I was doin' good with 7 kids of my own, but I shore ain't got no grandkids. 'Specially ain't got none what's ol' 'nuff to be married. You are married, ain'tcha sonny?"

"Yessir, I am," grinned Talon turning red around the collar, "but just recently. We've got a cabin up the canyon aways," motioning with a turn of his head.

"Well, whatever you do, you take good care o' her. Good wimmens hard to find in this hyar country. It's mighty hard livin' in these mountains, yessir, what with these Cheyenne and 'rapahos doin' what theys doin', though I cain't blame 'em much. My first wife was a 'rapaho, and after she died, I took me a wife from the Cheyenne. She was a tough one she was, she got her a notion one day she didn't want nuthin' to do with me no more an' she just up an' sets the kid and all my makins' outside the tipi and that was it. Quickest deevorce you ever did see. Yup, thats the way them Cheyenne wimmens is, they take a notion and yore out on yore ear faster'n you kin say Jack Squat! But I got me a good 'un this time. Didn't want no more Injuns so I got me a right nice little Mex gal.

She weren't but a pup when I married up with her, an' she done give me six more kids, three boys and three girls, an' theys the purtiest bunch a' kids you ever did see, even if'n I do say so, my ownself." He nodded his head to agree with himself and looked at Talon as he continued, "Say, younker, how 'bout you 'n me goin' over to the saloon yonder and throw us back a few? Ya wanna?"

"I've got a better idea, Mr. Carson," he was quickly interrupted by Carson sayin, "Kit, Kit, no Mister to it, just Kit."

Talon continued, "O.K. Kit, how 'bout you comin' back to the cabin with me and meet my wife and have supper with us?"

He looked at the young man and cocked his head to the side and replied, "You know, that's the best invitation I've had in a long time. I'd be mighty proud to come to supper with you and if yore wife's anything like your Grandma, I bet she's a doozy!"

With dinner over, the three sat back and enjoyed their coffee as Ginny continued to ply their guest with questions about his many exploits. When she learned that he and Talon's grandpa had been friends when they were young, she felt a special kinship with the man and wanted to know more about his life. "Mr. Car . . . I mean Kit, I've read several of the novels that were written about you. My friend, Mary Sue, and I used to read them and talk about the adventures you had and we wondered if we'd ever get to see some of the country you explored. They were so exciting, I especially liked the one that told about the time you had a duel with the French trapper to win your wife, the woman of the Arapaho. That was at a Rendevous, wasn't it?"

"Yes, missy, it was. That was a long time ago," he wistfully answered getting a bit of a glassy stare to him. "She's long gone now, and our little girl, Adeline, she's a married woman now. Ain't made me a granpa yet though, thank the Lord," he responded. "But now I've got a wonderful wife. I tell you she has put up with more of my gallavantin' around than any woman ought to, an' it seems like ever' time I come home, I got a new kiddo runnin' aroun', yessir, at last count it was all tied up at three and three."

"You mean to tell me you have 6 kids?" asked Ginny incredulously. This man didn't look like he was old enough or had lived long enough to have that many children.

"That's right, and they sure is the cutest lookin' rascals ya ever wanna see. Shore is a good thing they look like their Ma, though. Ain't a tow head in the bunch. They got her dark hair and dark brown eyes, but they got my chin and nose, poor kids."

"Would you tell us about one of your adventures, please?" asked Ginny, feeling like a little girl sitting before one of her real-life idols.

"Well, let me see. There was that time when, well it was durin' the Mexican American War an' ol' General Kearny wanted me to guide his outfit out to Californy. Wal, we was near San Pasqual, Californy and a whole bunch o' them Mex soldiers attacked and we was outnumbered 4 or 5 to one. Wal, we held out till night an' the gen'l sent a couple men to San Diego for reinforcements, but they wouldn't make it back in time, so we had to skedaddle 'fore them soldiers hit us in the mornin'. Wal, I told the Gen'l to have the men take off their shoes so we could sneak out, an we dun' it by gum. But the feller what was a carryin' the shoes, lost 'em!" He slapped his knee and cackled a laugh and continued. "We had to travel the rest o' the way cross prickly pear cactus and all them rocks a'barefoot! Heeheeeheee . . ."

"Well, what happened?" pleaded Ginny, hanging on every word.

"Wal, just what happens to any blamed fool that tries to cross a desert barefoot, we all died!" he said with a somber expression as he watched her reaction.

Her startled look caused her facial expression to melt from shock to laughter as she slapped at his elbow on the table. "You did not! Here you sit, lying like all the other men just like you!"

"Well, if we didn't die, we musta been saved by them reinforcements from San Diego. Just in time though, cuz I was thinkin' 'bout dyin', I was."

They said their good byes to the mountain man as he mounted to leave. They were standing arm in arm on the porch and Talon explained, "When you take the stage, I won't be Shotgun. My driver and I are usually on the Westbound toward Ft. Bridger. But, whenever you're back in the area, you are certainly welcome to our home."

"You know, that just might happen. The way I understand it, the army is wantin' me to take a post down South of here and help with the Utes. So, I might be back this way, and if I do, I'll sure look forward to some of your cookin', missy." He tipped his hat and reined his horse around as Talon and Ginny waved their good bye.

To The Overland Trail

Chapter Fourteen

Massacre

THE REVEREND COLONEL John Chivington sat comfortably in the saddle, leaning his forearm on the saddle horn with arms crossed, as he looked over the gathered troops, supply wagons, and cannon. He was pleased with what he saw, three cannons, ample supplies for a two-week campaign and 425 men of the 3rd Colorado Cavalry. Because the 3rd had never been in a conflict, they were known as the "Bloodless Third" and the men were anxious to shed that moniker.

Chivington looked to the junior officers and gave a nod to Captain Silas Soule to start the column. James Beckwourth, the noted frontiersman, had sold his services to the detachment and was to serve as their guide and scout to Fort Lyon and on to the Indian encampments. He expected the expedition would take three days and would arrive at Fort Lyon on November 27th, 1864. His estimation proved correct as they rode into the fort about mid-day on the 27th.

By the end of the day, Colonel Chivington had taken command of the 1st Colorado Cavalry from Major Scott Anthony, who would remain behind at the fort, and the remainder of the 1st Regiment New Mexico Volunteer Infantry. His total corps now numbered over 700 men. He directed the Sutler of the post to provide ample liquor to the men as they were going into battle on the coming day.

It wasn't a compassionate move but simply because Chivington believed when the men were well "oiled" they would be less resistant to orders and his plans for the Indians. Several of the men had additional flasks filled with whiskey to carry on their campaign and to fortify their courage.

The morning of the 28th, the men were not up to their usual precision and promptness, many suffering severe hangovers, but the column was ready to move out by mid-morning. The day's march brought them almost to the reservation and the camp of the Cheyenne. After making camp, the soldiers and militia gathered around the fires and began the usual bragging on what they would do the following day. Flasks were passed around and the celebration began.

Men with fear in their hearts often over compensate by drinking, carousing and participating in other revelry. Anything to take their minds off the doubts that assail the fearful and no man wanted to be branded a coward. Often bragging about what they want to do and are determined to do, the words would come back to motivate them to what they believed was greater bravery and exploits. The practice of one-up-manship made the rounds of the campfires as vulgarities were shared and action anticipated.

Chivington gathered his officers together around a campfire and as the men seated themselves on logs and stones, he shared Beckwourth's scouting report of the Indians camp. Using the ground and a stick, he drew a crude map and designated positions for the different companies and placement of the artillery. "We'll move out before first light and have the morning light to take our positions. We'll start with an artillery bombardment and then the designated companies will attack simultaneously at my order. There is to be no quarter given, every redskin must be killed. Am I understood?" asked the

Colonel, looking around the fire at each of his officers. Captain Silas Soule asked, "What about the women and children, are they to be killed also?"

"Remember the Hungate massacre? They raped and killed the woman and almost decapitated two little children. Can we do any less? Every redskin is to die! Nits make Lice, don't forget that!" barked Chivington in reply. "Now, anything else?"

There were no other questions but each of the somber faced men just nodded their heads in understanding.

"Fine, fine. Now, get your rest and be ready to teach those animals a lesson they'll never forget. We will not tolerate their continued depravity and murder!" The men rose quietly and made their way back to their bedrolls with the weight of command on their shoulders.

The site of the village was at the confluence of Eureka Creek and Big Sandy Creek, but unlike the name implies, there was little water in the creek bottoms except in early Spring runoffs. Chivington placed one battery of cannon and one company of troopers on the North edge of Eureka Creek, partially obscured by scattered and leafless cottonwoods.

The other two batteries of cannon and the remainder of troops were arrayed on a slight rise and in a half circle on the south and west sides of the village. The Cheyenne were rousing from their lodges and some had spotted the troops and the surprise and concern was evident with several women grabbing their children and retreating to the lodges.

When Black Kettle was told, he came from his lodge and looked around at the troops that were mounted and surrounding the village. He looked back at his lodge and walked toward it, motioning toward the American flag and the white flag beneath it trying to signal to the troops that this was a peaceful village.

Chivington gave the signal for the bombardment to begin and the two cannons roared to be echoed from across the village by the other battery. The resulting explosions from the shells immediately took their toll in both death and destruction. The people screamed and women grabbed children and ran in confusion in every direction.

White haired old men ducked into tipis to grab for bows and arrows, having surrendered their arms at Fort Lyon. Again, the cannon roared and the screams continued, a few were shouting for the others to run toward the upper reaches of Sand Creek. Chivington directed one cannon to concentrate on the village and the other to direct its fire toward the fleeing crowd and Sand Creek. He stood back and watched the exploding shells hail down their destructive explosions and grinned.

Looking from side to side, he raised his sabre above his head and catching the eyes of his officers he shouted, "Charge!" and lowered his sabre pointing toward the village as he spurred his mount.

Listening to his bugler sound the charge, his adrenaline surged and he leaned over the neck of his running horse feeling the mane and wind whipping at his face. Some of the hide lodges had already caught fire and the smoke from the cannon and the fires obscured his vision but he continued his charge.

An old man stepped from a lodge with an arrow notched and as he pulled the bowstring back, Chivington's sabre swept down and almost decapitated the man, whose body fell in a heap at the entrance of his lodge, only to be trampled by the cavalry mount. Choosing the personal attack with his sabre instead of his sidearm or a Springfield rifle, the Colonel looked for his next victim. Reining his horse between the lodges he spotted a woman fleeing with a bundle in her arms and he quickly overtook her without slowing his running horse. He slashed at the woman as he passed and watched as she fell with blood spurting from her neck. The bundle was a blanket wrapped baby that screamed when it hit the ground. Chivington did not slow his attack.

Other cavalrymen mimicked the charge of their leader but with sidearms or rifles blazing and they watched their victims fall. The infantry ran into the village and fired their rifles but continued their charge without reloading but using their rifles as clubs as they struck down anything that was before them.

One man dropped to one knee, reloaded his rifle and brought it up to take aim at his target. Running before him was a solitary toddler, trying its best to catch the others that ran from the village. The infantryman brought his rifle to his shoulder, took aim and squeezed off his shot, only to be disappointed when he missed. Again, he reloaded, aimed, fired and missed.

He was watched by another man that had two chevrons on his sleeve and was told, "Here trooper, let me show you how it's done!" He stood behind the man and took aim at the fleeing toddler that was now no more than forty feet distant, and fired, knocking the child to the ground. There was no movement and the men looked at one another as they realized what they had done, but were without remorse and grinned at one another when the corporal put his finger to his tongue and made a motion as if he was marking up one more kill.

The clamor of the attack continued with a deafening din as screams from the victims, explosions from trooper's weapons, cannon fire, shouted commands and more. The smoke and dust was choking and the noise deafening. Confusion was everywhere among the Indians and troopers alike. A trooper with three chevrons on his sleeve staggered between the lodges with a crazed look on his face and blood on his hands and arms, he brandished a Springfield with a bloody bayonet as he looked for more victims.

Two men were hunkered behind a lodge with a bloody squaw on the ground before them as their intentions were evident by their stance and actions. One held the woman's arms while another grabbed her legs as she kicked at them and screamed. An old man ran up behind the men and buried his hatchet in the head of the one at her feet then looked up as the other fired his pistol in his face. Death marched slowly among the lodges and swept his scythe in a broad sweeping arch taking everything in his path.

Chivington reined his horse around to take another pass through the village and spotted several men giving chase to the fleeing villagers toward Sand Creek. He scanned the slight rise to the south of the village and was surprised to see several mounted men still in place above the village.

At the head of one company was Captain Silas Soule who had refused to be a part of the massacre and told his men of Company D to hold their fire. Lieutenant Joseph Cramer, commanding company K of the 1st Colorado Cavalry likewise kept his men from the battle. They were witnessing the carnage and the depravity of the men they had counted as friends and compatriots.

As the battle waned, Chivington rode among the bodies and lodges noting several of his troopers were among the dead. However, he was pleased to see the number of dead bodies that lay scattered throughout the remains of the village.

Bodies of all sizes and ages were bloodied and mutilated by the carnage. Some had been dismembered by the cannon fire, others had been maimed by the battle and the troopers. The American flag and the white flag snapped in the wind, catching Chivington's attention. He looked at them and rode to the tipi and with one swipe of his bloody sabre cut the rope and dropped the flag to the ground. Leaving it lay in the dust, he spurred his mount away from the carnage and onto the slight rise from which the battle began.

When Black Kettle heard the shouted warning, he quickly exited his lodge and looked around. He was surprised to see several hundred blue coats apparently surrounding his village. He quickly shouted and motioned toward the flag to indicate this was a peaceful village, but within moments, the cannon roared and he knew they were under attack.

His first thought was that he had sent almost all the warriors on a hunt for buffalo. When he was told the soldiers would no longer supply the promised provisions, he knew his village must have meat for the coming winter and sent his men in search of buffalo. Now there were no warriors, just old men and women and children. There was no one to fight back but the old men with bows and arrows.

Several of the old chiefs had joined Black Kettle and had enjoyed the time without war, but it was a short time and now they were faced with attack. Black Kettle ducked into his lodge to get his bow and arrows and grabbed his war lance and shield as well. He slipped the quiver over his head and shoulder, strung the bow, readied himself with a quick prayer to the Great Spirit and stepped from his lodge.

He was greeted by a charging cavalryman with a pistol. The man fired at Black Kettle and the chief heard the bullet whip past his ear as he leaned forward with his lance grasped in both hands and drove it into the side of the blue coat, unseating him from his horse. The blue coat dropped just past Black Kettle's lodge and the Indian stepped to his side to ensure he would kill no more of his people as he slit his throat and took his scalp. Tucking the white man's hair under his belt he looked around at the confused people running from charging soldiers and seeking escape. He saw White Horse, a young mother, fall when a bullet struck her in the leg, but she rose and stumbled toward Sand Creek.

Another woman, who had proven herself a warrior after being a captive, Coyote Howling, let loose an arrow that quickly found its mark in the chest of a charging blue coat. She quickly notched another arrow and looked for another target. Black Kettle motioned for her to flee to Sand Creek and protect the others. She nodded her head in acceptance as Black Kettle smiled at the woman who had been called Mary Shipley when she was captured as a very young woman so many years ago. She had proven herself to be a good warrior after her man, White Buffalo, who was the shaman for the village, had been killed by the blue coats. She now sought vengeance for his death.

After quickly surveying the massacre, Black Kettle took off at a trot to join the few that had escaped to Sand Creek. When he arrived, just ahead of a pursuing blue coat, he was surprised when Coyote Howling let loose an arrow that passed by his head but buried itself in the neck of his pursuer.

He looked back and saw the man fall then turned to nod his head at Coyote Howling. She nodded her head in return and walked up the creek bed to join the others. They were busy digging into the banks of the creek to make some shelter and protection for themselves. Black Kettle watched at George Bent, the son of William Bent and Little Flower, helped a woman and her child fit herself into the dugout protection of the sandy bank. The chief looked back in the direction of the village as the din of the battle lessened and soon grew quiet. An occasional shot from a pistol was heard and the chief knew the blue coats were killing the wounded. A few women and children were taken captive, but were later murdered at the hands of the drunken soldiers.

By late afternoon, Black Kettle knew the soldiers were gone and together with a few volunteers, he returned to the village.

As he walked among the remains of the lodges, tears began to dim his vision but he did not waver in his task. He and the others checked everybody for any sign of life and gathered anything that would help them in their journey from this place. He staggered when he saw the mutilated body of a woman he recognized as a young mother that was close to delivery of her second child. Her belly had been cut open and the baby removed and lay beside her in a puddle of blood.

The woman had been stabbed repeatedly and scalped and the baby had his head caved in by a blow of some kind. He passed others, women and small children that had been mutilated. Several of the women and men had their genitals removed in the mutilation and were scalped. Fingers, ears and even noses were cut off some of the bodies. Black Kettle shook his head as he remembered the remonstrances of Governor

Evans for the mutilation of some whites that had been killed in battle with the Cheyenne and Arapaho. He had called it barbaric and Black Kettle wondered what the good governor would call this betrayal and massacre.

To The Overland Trail

Chapter Fifteen

Friends

MARY SUE AND GINNY were seated together in the restaurant at Aunt Sophie's in LaPorte. The two friends were chattering on about everything imaginable when they overheard a couple at a nearby table mention Chivington's massacre. Ginny turned toward them and "Pardon me, did you say something about a massacre?"

The man at the table who was well attired and known as an attorney in town faced his questioner and said, "Yes, you did. Have you not heard about the big Indian battle?"

"Why no, would you share the news with us? We'd really like to know," replied Ginny.

"Well, it seems that the Reverend Colonel took his troops against a village of the Cheyenne and wiped them out. The only trouble is, his account of the battle and the accounts of others that were there are quite different," the attorney turned his chair to face the ladies and continued, "Chivington said they killed as many as five or six hundred warriors and stated emphatically that our Indian problem was over. But some of his subordinate officers, and I don't remember their names right off, said it was an unarmed village of old men and women and children. One account says there were only about 20 to 30 warriors and over 100 women and children that were killed. Some of the troopers were even showing around body parts of their victims as trophies of their bravery," he shook his head in disgust at the image.

"Oh my, that's dreadful!" said Mary Sue. "And if that's true, I believe he just aggravated the Indian problem instead of ending it."

"My sentiments exactly. That's all we needed was a bunch of angry Indians seeking vengeance on our communities. Chivington ought to be taken out and shot," stated the attorney.

"Well, thank you sir for sharing that news, dreadful though it is," said Mary Sue as she turned back to her table and Ginny. Mary was surprised to see Ginny looking at a man standing in the doorway and looking around as if he was searching for someone.

When she saw him look her way, Ginny motioned for him to join them. When the buckskin clad man saw her wave her hand, he smiled and moved to join them at their table. Ginny turned to Mary Sue and said, "Mary Sue, may I present Mr. Kit Carson." Mary Sue looked at the man and back at Ginny and back at the man, smiled and said, "Pleased to meet you, Mr. Carson. Won't you join us?"

"I'd be happy to m'am. I was lookin' fer Talon, Miss Ginny, but ol' Porter over at the station said he was out on a run but that he'd seen you come in here. So, I thought I better at least say Howdy 'fore I moved on."

"Well, I'm certainly glad you did, and yes, Talon is out on a run but he should be back tomorrow. Are you leaving soon?" asked Ginny.

"Well, I'm actually headed back later today, seems th' army just cain't get along without me. They want to make me a Brevet Brigadier General, can you imagine that?"

"A general? Well, congratulations General Carson," said Ginny with a smile. She suddenly had a thought about the earlier conversation and now asked, "Well, General sir, what can you tell us about the great battle of Colonel Chivington? We've heard there are different accounts about it."

A look of disgust crossed his face as he crossed his arms and rested his elbows on the table and started, "Jist to think of that dog Chivington and his dirty hounds, down thar at Sand Creek's 'nuff to make any man sick. His men shot down squaws and blew the brains out of little innocent children. You call sich soldiers Christians, do ye? And Indians savages? What der yer s'pose our Heavenly Father, who made both them and us, thinks of these things? I tell you what, I don't like a hostile red skin any more than you do. And when they are hostile, I've fought 'em, hard as any man. But I never yet drew a bead on a squaw or papoose, and I despise the man who would. Pardon me ladies fer bein' so blunt, but them things just rile me sum'thin fearful."

"And well they should, Kit. What you describe is definitely an atrocity and no man can call himself Christian that would do that," said Ginny.

"General, would you like to order some lunch? We just placed our order for the lunch special, some ham and beans and cornbread, would you like some as well?" asked Mary Sue.

The three enjoyed their lunch together and Mary Sue was as taken with Carson as Ginny had been on his first visit. Ginny had told her friend about the time with Carson and she was amazed with the stories and tales that were shared. Now she marveled at the man that sat before her and his congenial attitude and confident manner.

Ginny broke Mary Sue's reverie when she asked Carson, "General," and was interrupted by Carson with a reminder to call him Kit, "Kit, then, I was just thinking about what you said about Chivington claiming to be Christian and I remembered you saying you left the Presbyterian Church when you married Josefa, is that right?"

"Yes m'am. Her family is an old and very wealthy family and they've been a part of the Catholic church for generations.

To join the church was required if I wanted to make Josefa my bride and long 'bout then, I'da done jist about any'thin' for her to be my wife," he grinned at the thought.

"My family has been a part of the Presbyterian church what seems like forever too. But when you said that I was reminded about what Talon told me one time. He said, 'It's not what church or religion you are a part of, it's what relationship you have with Jesus. He should be your personal Savior no matter what church you belong to,' and he went on to tell me what the Bible says about the plan of salvation. That everyone is a sinner and the penalty for that sin is death and hell forever.

But Jesus paid the price for our sins on the cross and all we have to do is pray and ask Him for the gift of eternal life, and He'll give us the free gift of salvation. So, he told me about a simple prayer and to just admit to God that I'm a sinner, and that I want his forgiveness and to ask for the gift of salvation and God would give it to me. So right there, out in the wilderness where the Indians were chasin' us, I prayed and accepted that gift of eternal life and I've been happy ever since." She paused a moment and looked at Carson and asked, "Have you ever done that, Kit? I mean pray and ask Jesus to save you from that penalty of death and hell?"

"Uh, well, I've prayed before," and he chuckled at the thought, "usually when I'm in a heap o' trouble. But I don't think I've ever prayed like that. A free gift, huh? All I gotta do is pray and ask for it?" he asked as he looked at the young women at the table.

Both women nodded their heads in agreement and Mary Sue added, "I did that too, but I was a lot younger. You see, Kit, God loves us so much He sent his only son to pay the price for our sins so we don't have to, but we have to accept his gift. It's not just believing in God, most people do, but it's personally taking responsibility for our sins and knowing we can't pay for them. When we truly want to be certain of Heaven as our eternal home and we're willing to accept His payment, then He will gladly give us that gift. If you would like, we can all pray together, right here and right now."

He looked at the women and was moved by their sincerity and concern, then looked around at the others in the restaurant and said, "Ladies, I'ma thankin' you for what you told me and I'm sure I'll be doin' whatchu said. But I'm a private man, an' I'd rather be doin' my prayin' when I'm by myself."

Ginny smiled at Carson and reached out to touch his hand as she said, "Of course, I understand completely. We just wanted you to know what we believe to be so important and that's the eternal welfare of your soul." She drew her hand back and smiled and changed the subject.

"So, Kit, when are you going to decide about this General thing?" asked Ginny.

He was relieved at the change in the conversation and grinned when he answered, "First thang, I gotta talk to Josefa 'bout it. I'm not shore she's up to me bein' gone again, but Ft. Garland ain't too far from home, so mebbe so. We'll just have to wait n' see. The army thinks I might help 'em with the Utes."

"Talon's family is friendly with the Utes, as a matter of fact, one of the men that came out with them from St. Louis, married one of the Ute women and they live together on the ranch. From what Talon has said, the Ute leaders often visit at the ranch and they've even fought the Cheyenne together."

"Is that a fact? Well, that's good to know. I might have to call on your husband to help me out."

"Now, don't you go taking my husband away from home. If we ever leave here, we'll be together and he won't be a wanderer like you've been, at least not without me along," replied Ginny as she smiled at the Pathfinder.

Carson bid his good byes and told Ginny to give his greetings to Talon which she readily agreed to do, then he tipped his hat and left the restaurant.

Mary Sue looked at Ginny and said, "You were certainly right about him. He is fascinating." Ginny nodded her head in agreement as she watched Carson leave.

Chapter Sixteen

Gathering

WHEN COYOTE HOWLING returned from her scout of the camp, she reported to Black Kettle, "The blue coats have returned and destroyed or taken everything. Nothing remains and no one lives."

Her report confirmed what Black Kettle had previously discovered, but he hoped there would be something left to recover, for the survivors had a long journey before them. He had conferred with the only other surviving chiefs, Sand Hill and Left Hand, and they agreed those that remain must go to the camps in the Smoky Hill area.

They urged the survivors to begin the journey toward the many camps between the Smoky Hill River and the Republican River. The bands that had refused to join Black Kettle and White Antelope and the others that sought peace at Fort Lyon had fled to the North and established their camps between these rivers. Now the survivors would seek comfort and aid from these Cheyenne, Arapaho and Sioux.

Although many of the band's horses had been captured by the blue coats, several had been taken by fleeing members of the band. Many of those returned to find the straggling survivors and began to offer their help. The extra mounts were given to the chiefs and the few warriors, such as Coyote Howling and Bear Claw. Black Kettle sent these two warriors ahead to scout the trail and to warn of any dangers or blue coats.

Dusk of the second day traveling brought them to the first village of the Smoky Hill area. The villagers were quick to offer aid and many of the survivors chose to remain with this band, but others were determined to continue and find other bands and perhaps be reunited with friends and family. The villages were scattered but within a day's travel of one another. Most were Arapaho and Cheyenne, but there were also Sioux that had allied themselves through the influence of the Dog Soldier bands that continued to make war against the whites.

Word quickly spread of the ruthless slaughter of the people and the chiefs that had sought peace and now many, like the great warrior Roman Nose, turned their back on those that still wanted peace and joined the Dog Soldiers. The war pipe was smoked and passed among the villages and a council was called to determine the will and the path of the people.

In the past, the council of Forty-Four Chiefs determined the course of the people, but now many of those had been killed. As the surviving chiefs and others joined the council, all looked around to see who was absent. Many of the revered elders and chiefs were missing, White Antelope, One Eye, Yellow Wolf, Big Man, War Bonnet, Bear Man, Spotted Crow and Bear Robe had all been killed.

Now the traditional system of leadership by the council was changed and the more militant young warriors cried for revenge and war. Roman Nose rose and all eyes turned toward this respected warrior as he began, "Many of our elders walk with the spirits on this day. They sought peace with the white men and were given death," he spat the words like arrows from a strong bow, "and if we do not give them vengeance, we too will walk beside them!"

At that declaration, the younger warriors shouted their agreement and cried for war. He remained standing and lifted his arms for their attention, "I have long believed the only way we could defeat the whites is for us to be agreed," he waved his hand to those in the circle and beyond, "and now we have our brothers the Arapaho, and the Sioux, who have joined us in this fight. Now, if we can gather more of our brothers until we have as many warriors as will cover this plain," he motioned to the flats of the land around them, "we can rid our land of these whites that have the blood of our people on their hands!"

As many shouted and beat the ground with their war clubs, Roman Nose seated himself to wait for others to speak.

Black Kettle rose to his feet and waited for silence. His somber expression told of deep sadness as he began, "The spirits of my people cry from the other side in sorrow for their families that remain. My heart is heavy with grief at what I have seen and my people have known. I still long for a time when our people will know peace and fear only hunger or cold but can still sleep in their lodges without fear of the coming of death. I still believe there will be a time that we can live together with the whites," he was interrupted by many of the young warriors that shouted their angry disagreement but he lifted his hands to continue, "but I also know, we must have revenge for what has been done." Those that had shouted their derision now looked at one another and grinned at what they knew would soon come.

Chief Neva of the Arapaho stood and began, "We are together with our brothers, the Cheyenne and the Sioux, and when we go to battle with the whites, our people will shed the blood of those that killed so many at Sand Creek. I say we fight together and when our numbers are great, our revenge will be great! I say we send riders to the villages beyond this river," he motioned toward the distant Republican River to the North, "and bring more of our people together and we can show the whites they cannot do this to our people. And if

Black Kettle still wants peace, he can tell the whites that remain, if any, what they must do to have that peace instead of listening to their demands."

Black Wolf of the Dog Soldiers stood and the response among the young warriors was one of shouted encouragement, but Black Wolf raised his hands to speak and began, "I am Black Wolf of the Dog Soldiers. We have had many raids against the white man and we have seen victory, but we have also had many losses. There are many of the whites that run and wet themselves when they see us coming," most of those present laughed at his description and he grinned but continued, "but there are also many warriors among them. They have rifles that shoot far, farther than any we have, and rifles that shoot many times before reloading. Those rifles make one man as if he were this many," he thrust his open hand before them indicating the number five, "and to fight them we must have many warriors and we must have some of these weapons. To do that, we must strike in many places, the stage stations, the ranches, the villages, even the white man's forts! What we want to do will take every warrior we have and more."

He turned to Roman Nose and spoke again, "And I say we have our greatest warrior, Roman Nose, lead us in this battle!" All the warriors shouted their agreement and waved their war clubs over their heads to show their eagerness to go to war.

As Black Wolf was seated, the old chiefs looked to one another and with a slight nod, agreed that the mantle of leadership was passing. Roman Nose stood and said, "If it is the will of this council that I become the war leader, I will accept that role. But if that is to be, we must agree to stop all raids and gather all our warriors so we can attack in force."

After the council was completed, the agreement had been made to make Roman Nose the war leader and that word would be sent to all the known villages of the Cheyenne, Arapaho, and Sioux to rally as many warriors as possible. Black Kettle, Neva, Sand Hill, Left Hand, Heap of Buffalo and others gathered in Black Kettle's lodge with Roman Nose and discussed the plan for the coming war. They knew it would take three to six weeks for the villages to respond and join them, but they wanted to have a plan ready for all to become involved. They were planning a war against the whites to exact their revenge and all wanted the toll to be great.

Chapter Seventeen

East

HENRY PORTER, THE LAPORTE Station Keeper, leaned his elbows on the counter as he looked at Talon and Bull seated by the pot-belly stove with coffee cups in hand. He continued, "So, I guess you fellas make quite an impression on our superintendent, Hugo Richards, when he rode with you a while back. I think it was when you found Cooper Creek burned. Anyway, since the ruckus with Chivington, he's thinkin' there might be some trouble with the Injuns to the East of here so he's changin' the schedule and wants our best fellas on that route."

Talon looked at Bull and over his shoulder to Porter and asked, "You mean to tell me he wants us on that run? Is that cuz we're so good or cuz he thinks we're expendable?" Bull snorted at his comment and shook his head.

"No, no, you're not ex . . . ex . . . or whatever it was you said. He thinks you two are the best! Since Holladay changed the route at the Fort Morgan cutoff and made it go through Denver, it's been better. But ol' Chivington has ordered us to bypass Denver and go back to the route through Latham and such. He said the way you fellas handled yourselves when you came through there made him confi . . . con . . . consarn it! Anyhow he thinks you fellas can do just 'bout anything."

"So, now what?" asked Bull.

"So, you two will be on the east bound route. Now, I know from here to Julesburg is a three-day run, an if'n you go all the way, you'll be a pair o' tired ol' goats, but you can take a day off 'fore ya head back. That'll make a full week. Then you can take a full week off 'fore you have to do it again. But ol' Richards might change his mind an' go back to shorter runs by then. Ya cain't never tell 'bout these big shots, ya' know," surmised Porter.

"So, when do we start this new schedule, anyway?" asked Talon.

"First thing Monday morn' an' if'n ever'thin' goes right, you'll be back right'chere on Sunday even'in," answered Porter. Talon looked at Bull and the big man shrugged his shoulders and said, "Ya' better bring yore buffler coat, cuz them winds on the flats can get plum mizzable."

Talon shook his head at the task facing the two and replied, "What we're gonna need is sum'thin ta' keep the arrows outta our backside!"

Bull stood and let a "Hummmppph" escape to show his disgruntled attitude, but motioned to his Shotgun to join him and suggested, "Let's go git us some fresh coffee at the restaurant. This mud's chokin' my gizzard."

Seated at a table in Aunt Sophie's, Talon smiled at Mary Sue as she poured the coffee for the men. He said, "Thanks, Mary Sue. Say, while you're here, me'n Bull are gonna be on a different schedule startin' Monday which means we'll be gone a little longer an' I'd appreciate it if you or little Johnny could check on Ginny durin' the week. I mean, you don't have to do it your own self, but if you could have somebody check on her from time to time, I'd be mighty grateful."

She smiled at him and said, "Sure, Talon. I'll have 'little' Johnny, as you called him, who by the way is growin' like a weed and is almost as tall as I am, but I'll have him ride up and check on her. He'd think that would make him almighty important too."

As Mary Sue walked away from the table, Bull asked Talon, "She the other'n that you brung back from the Injuns?"

"Yup, her and her brother, little Johnny. Good people. Mary Sue saw her daddy killed and her momma shot with an arrow through her chest, but her momma didn't die till after they brought her here to LaPorte, but Mary Sue and them were already with the Cheyenne."

Bull looked at Mary Sue as she busied herself with the other customers and shook his head, "Musta been purty tough on the little ladies an' boy, bein' with the Injuns like that."

"Yeah, but they weren't treated too badly, coulda been a lot worse," replied Talon.

Bull looked back at Talon and asked, "So, you've been over that stretch of road 'tween here an' Julesburg, then?"

"Not the whole thing, just from Beaver Creek station thisaway."

"Purty flat country ain't it?"

"Most of it, lot like the stretch from Elk Mountain to North Platte. You know, sage brush, gramma grass, rollin' hills and lots of antelope. But I'm thinkin' from Beaver Creek on West to Julesburg is flatter still, 'course I ain't seen it yet."

The men finished their coffee and parted with neither one looking forward to this new assignment. What had gone unsaid was the greater risk of Indian attack. That part of the Overland Trail was right through the midst of the lands previously claimed by the Cheyenne and Arapaho and most of the Eastern plains were still claimed by them.

After Chivington's attack, there had been no more raids by the Indians, but no one expected the Cheyenne or the Arapaho to seek after peace. Their nature had always been one of retaliation for any attack and most were expecting some type of reprisal.

The first day on the new route was a long one, but without incident. When the stage pulled into the station at Bijou Creek, both Bull and Talon were hungry and tired and looking forward to a long night's rest. The two men eagerly downed two helpings of the beef stew and after Talon took a reconnoiter walk around the station both turned in for the evening. They rolled out their bedrolls in a pair of empty stalls in the barn and were soon competing with one another as they sawed logs in their sleep.

The second day of the route saw stops at Junction and Beaver Creek with the latter being their noon meal stop. The team was switched out for a six-up of mules. From Beaver Creek to Julesburg, the roadway had many sandy stretches and the pulling was more difficult. Experience had shown the mules fared far better with the sandy soil pulling and the stations were stocked with nothing but mules for this almost eighty-mile stretch of rolling hills and dry land traveling.

After the change at Beaver Creek, Bull shouted "Ándele!" and snapped the reins to start the afternoon's travel. With only one swing station, American Ranch or Kelly's, between them and their last stop of the day at Valley, both men were hopeful of an uneventful trip.

Chapter Eighteen

Procession

THE COLD WIND WHISTLED in from the Northeast as Bull and Talon turned up collars and pulled down on their floppy felt hats to shield their faces from winter's blast. Talon wrapped his woolen scarf over the top of his hat and tucked it in his thick buffalo coat to protect his face and neck from what felt like airborne icicles. The tempest had come suddenly but not totally unexpected for they had kept their eyes on the foreboding clouds all day and watched as they blackened and boiled towards them.

Even in the midst of a storm, Talon's job was to be ever vigilant for any danger and although the possibility of Indian attack was minimal, nothing could be taken for granted. Talon peeked from under the brim of his hat and looked toward the river where he thought he saw movement. He straightened in his seat and looked directly at the break in the cottonwoods that lined the bank of the South Platte. Even with the moving coach, Talon could see where a tangle of driftwood shielded the sandy island and a procession of Indians were making their way across the shallow waters of the crossing.

He elbowed Bull and pointed. The big man snapped his head in that direction to see what appeared to be an entire village of Arapaho making their way to the edge of the trees. Bull slapped the reins to the mules to hurry their progress. He turned to Talon and said, "I think we can make it without them comin' after us. They're too busy gettin' cross the river." His words were shouted to be heard over the howling winds. Talon nodded his head and craned to watch the crossing, although most were now shielded by the tree lined bank. He guessed they were making the crossing before making camp. This late in the day and with a storm rising, they would probably camp within the cover of the trees.

The mules leaned to their task and quickened their pace but the pulling was a challenge with the sandy soil of the trail. The animals liked the cold wind even less than the men, but their blinders provided some protection and the mules ducked and turned their heads as they valiantly trudged on at a canter. Another hour of fighting the blistering wind brought the stage to Kelly's station, also known as American Ranch. The two passengers, both drummers, made a bee line to the privy while Bull and Talon went into the station to warm up.

The station's primary purpose was as a ranch and had become a stop on the stage line simply due to location. The line built bigger barns and corrals to handle the teams, and the Morris family readily fulfilled the responsibility of providing meals and accommodations for the travelers. The ranch had always been a favorite stop for the drivers and shotguns alike, but had never been designated a home station, so the overnight stops were seldom.

Bull and Talon, wanting to meet their schedule, returned to the coach and mounted up for the last leg of their route for the day. Valley station was the designated home station and was to be their stop for the night. With the cold wind increasing and the clouds threatening snow, they wanted to make the last fifteen miles before dark. The winter days were short on daylight and the dark clouds of the storm were robbing the travelers of much needed travel time.

With another "Ándele" from Bull, they were soon on their way. The fresh team, not appreciating being taken from the warm stall in the barn, reluctantly leaned into their task. Mules usually tended to be smarter than horses and seemed to be trying to tell the Jehu that what they were doing wasn't the best choice, but they yielded to the crack of Talon's encouraging whip.

With just a few miles behind them, the bottom dropped out of the storm clouds and they found themselves in a winter white out. The snow licked at every piece of exposed flesh as the storm became a horizontal assault. The team leaned into their traces with heads bowed, totally trusting the Jehu to guide them through the white wall. Bull could only peek from beneath the brim of his hat to occasionally catch a glimpse of the flat of the roadway, revealed only by the mounds of snow that marked the sagebrush beside the trail. He knew they were in trouble, but their only choice was to continue. He elbowed Talon and hollered over the howling winds, "Watch for a place of shelter where we can stop!"

"Yeah, but the hostler back at Kelly's told me there's another ranch not too far that we might be able to make, Godfrey's I think he said," answered Talon from under his woolen scarf that struggled to keep his hat secure. Their visibility was so hindered, they couldn't see the pair of leaders at the head of the team. Occasionally the wind would lessen as if to gain greater momentum and at those times they could catch a glimpse of the trail ahead or the trees off to their left about fifty yards that marked the river.

"There!" shouted Talon as he pointed forward and to the right of the road. He had a quick glimpse of buildings and motioned for Bull to make for the designated point. Within moments rising from the white were the vague outlines of three buildings and what appeared as a fortified wall.

Bull negotiated the mules through the gateway and pulled up before a large barn. The big door opened revealing two men shielding their faces as they watched the coach pull to a stop. The men quickly went to work to unhitch the mules as Bull and Talon stepped down from the box and went to the doors to instruct the passengers to disembark. An older man with a long white beard that was encrusted with snow hollered at the men and motioned them to the main house, "Go on in the house, the wife'll fix ya' sumpin' to eat and you can thaw out by the fire. Go 'head on, we'll take care o' the team!" he hollered over the wail of the wind.

It was a restless night for the two men as the skeletal fingers of the wailing winds clawed at every shuttered window of the house that held the passengers and the driver and shotgun. As the storm let up in the early hours of the morning, Talon and Bull enjoyed a few hours of rest but were soon awakened by the busy household. Light pried its way through the shutters and the men quickly dressed and joined the others at the table. Mrs. Godfrey provided an ample breakfast of eggs, bacon, biscuits and gravy as the men fortified themselves for the coming day. With a longer day before them, having to make up for the lost time between Godfrey's and Valley station, the men downed their meal and readied themselves for the day.

The bright blue of the cloudless sky arched in sharp contrast to the previous day's storm and the drifted snow around them. The unfinished wall of Godfrey's ranch acted like a drift fence that captured the blown snow in sculpted shapes as if some talented artist had used his brush to turn angles into arches. A bitter cold had plunged the temperature well below zero as the coach departed from Godfrey's ranch but Talon and Bull had borrowed a woolen quilt that now covered their laps and provided a degree of added comfort.

The white fingers of snowdrifts that marked the roadway did nothing to slow the mules and the deep cold and penetrating moisture had hardened the otherwise sandy soil, making the roadway harder and easier to travel. They made good time and as dusk threatened the end of the day, the coach pulled into Julesburg with exhausted mules and relieved men looking for at least a night of rest.

To The Overland Trail

Chapter Nineteen

Christmas

THE STAGE PULLED INTO the LaPorte station two days before Christmas, 1864. Ginny stood waiting for her man with Smokey at her side and her Henry cradled in her arms. She was bundled in her wool capote made from a Hudson Bay three-point blanket and she was a picture for Talon's memory. His broad smile told of his anticipation of seeing and greeting his wife.

Bull elbowed him and said, "Thar she is boy, now git yoreself on down there an' greet her proper."

Talon needed no further encouragement as the coach drew to a stop and the horses pranced, shaking their harness and trace chains as if they knew this was the end of their run. Smokey stood and wiggled his stub of a tail, anxious for his master's hand. The stage still rocked when Talon jumped down from the box and his two long strides brought him to Ginny, encompassing her with his arms and smothering her with a long-awaited kiss. She stood on tiptoes as she wrapped her arms around his neck, having stood her Henry against the post beside her. Station keeper, hostler, and Jehu all paused to jealously watch the young lovers greet one another.

Talon drew back, looked at Ginny with a broad smile, hugged her again and said, "It sure is good to see you."

She nodded her head in agreement and replied, "I'm glad you made it back in time for Christmas. This one is special since it'll be our first one together," she said as she flashed a coy smile at her husband. "And I've invited Mary Sue and Johnny to join us, after all they're practically family, you know."

"That's fine, and I've invited Bull to join us too. I think it'll be a fine Christmas. Oh, and just outside of town, we spotted a flock of turkey and I bagged a couple for our Christmas dinner!" declared Talon, proudly.

Ginny clapped her hands together and said, "Wonderful! Mary Sue will help me fix it and it'll be a great Christmas."

Talon grinned and stepped back up to the driver's box and retrieved his rifles, bedroll, haversack and the turkeys, dropping the roll, sack and turkeys to the boardwalk beside Ginny. As he stepped down he said to Bull, "Now don't forget Bull, Christmas day at our house!"

"Oh, I'll be thar, you can count on that," replied the Jehu.

When they arrived at the cabin, Talon busied himself putting up the horses and throwing some grass hay gathered in the fall. All the tack was stored in the shed and he carried the other gear to join Ginny in the cabin.

As he opened the door, he saw Ginny standing and grinning as she watched his reaction. He looked around and his eyes rested on the Christmas tree standing in the corner. A bushy blue spruce was decorated with her hand made colored chain garland. Other lovingly fashioned ornaments in the shape of balls, boxes, snowflakes, stars, and bells were carefully hung in an orderly arrangement throughout the tree. A larger star with some sort of sparkling decoration adorned the top of the tree. Talon smiled as he thought of the effort expended by his wife to make this a special time and held out his arms to invite her near. As she walked toward him he said, "That's the purtiest Christmas tree I ever did see! You are amazing Ginny!"

"Do you really like it?" she implored, seeking his approval.

"Like it? I love it!" he said as he wrapped her in his arms and held her close. She snuggled up against him and said, "I've missed you."

"And I've missed you too, but we're together now and we're gonna have a great Christmas!" he declared. He stacked his haversack, bedroll and rifles in the corner and turned to join his wife at the table. He let a sly grin cross his face as he thought of the contents of his bedroll and haversack, the surprise gifts for his wife and friends.

Many of the stations on the Overland Trail served as social gathering places and supply points for trappers, travelers, and wagon trains. Before the increase in conflict with the Cheyenne and Arapaho, many of the stations were also trading posts where the natives traded hides, pelts and crafts for their needed supplies. One of the more popular stations was Bijou Creek that still served any and all travelers and it was there that Talon successfully secured the gifts that now lay hidden in his gear.

"Mary Sue and Johnny will come out tomorrow so she can help with the dinner, she's much better at cooking than I am and I'm sure both you and Bull will appreciate that," she said with a smile.

"Now woman, you know I like your cooking and Bull said it was some of the best vittles he ever had, so don't be thinkin' you ain't appreciated," said Talon as he reached for her hand.

She had brewed them a cup of tea, an unusual treat, and she brought the cup to her lips and sipped the comforting brew. "Oh, I know you like my cooking and you appreciate what I do, but Christmas is special and I want our first one to be extra special, so Mary Sue will help and I'm sure it'll be great," she explained.

119

Talon smiled and nodded his head in agreement as he sipped his tea, knowing any argument would benefit no one.

"So, tell me about your trip. Was it exciting? Anything special happen?" quizzed Ginny.

"Oh, nothin' special, a little wind is all, but not bad," replied Talon, not wanting to alarm his wife about the Indians and the perils of traveling in winter. What she didn't know about, she couldn't worry about and he certainly didn't want his wife spending her days worrying when there was no need.

Christmas day came with blue skies devoid of clouds and snow. Had there been any greenery it could have been mistaken for a typical spring day. The women were busy with breakfast for everyone and Talon returned from his usual time of prayer at his special place in the woods, a habit formed at his father's side during his life at the ranch. Ginny welcomed him to the table with a kiss on the cheek and poured him a cup of coffee. His plate was filled with a slice of sugar cured ham buried under sourdough biscuits and gravy. Johnny sat at his side and as soon as the "Amen" was said after the prayer of thanks, he dug into his plateful of anticipated goodness.

Talon leaned back in his chair with one hand resting on the table near the handle of his coffee cup and looking at the women busily working at the counter preparing dishes for the dinner and said, "Say, this is Christmas, isn't it?" as if it had just dawned on him what day it was.

"Of course, it is silly, why do you think we're doing all this," said Ginny as she motioned to the scattered vegetables and dishes.

"Well, I thought Christmas was all about presents, and I don't see any," answered Talon as he feigned surprise as he looked at the tree.

"Well, smarty, I didn't see you with any presents in your arms," stated Ginny as she returned to her preparations.

Talon rose from his seat and said, "Wait a minute, what's this I see?" and bent down to reach far under the tree near the wall. He dragged out several packages he had placed there in the night and looked at them and said, "Lookee here, why this'ns for Johnny!" and handed the rectangular package to the young man whose wide eyes told of his surprise.

The women wiped their hands on their aprons and stepped nearer the bearer of gifts.

"And this one's for Ginny!" handing a sizable, soft package to his wife. She accepted it with a smile and waited as he looked at another package.

"This one's for Mary Sue," he said as he handed her a small wrapped package.

"Oh, and here's another for Ginny," as he handed the last package to his wife. He was seated on the floor and reached for his Bible that sat on the corner of a nearby shelf. "But before any of you can open them, there's something we need to do."

He opened the Bible and leafed through several pages and stopped at the second chapter of Luke and began to read with verse 1, "And it came to pass . . ." and continued through verse 20 " . . . praising God for all the things that they had heard and seen, as it was told unto them." "That's the real story of Christmas, how Christ was born unto us to become our Savior."

Talon sat the Bible down and said, "O.K. Johnny, why don't you show us what you got for Christmas?"

The boy eagerly tore into his package and when he recognized what it was he exclaimed, "Wow, Talon! It's a Bowie Knife! Thanks!" He turned it over and over and examined the scabbard and admired the deer horn handle and held it like a treasure.

With a nod from Talon, Mary Sue carefully opened her package and was thrilled to see a tortoise shell hair comb with an exquisitely carved floral design on the exposed portion. A tear came into her eye as she lifted her face to Talon and Ginny that now stood by his side and said, "It's beautiful, so like the one my mother had," she clutched it to her chest and said, "I'll treasure this, it is so beautiful. Thank you."

"Now it's your turn, girl, open 'em up. Do this one first," he said as he pointed to the larger one. She sat down and with the package on her lap, she opened it to find a pair of Indian made, high-top moccasins with warm rabbit fur lining. The soles were of buffalo hide and the tops were of elk hide. A beaded floral pattern covered the toes and the front of the tall tops. She "ooooed" and "awwwwwed" as she put her hands inside and then held the moccasins up for all to see. She quickly put them on and exclaimed, "They fit and they're so cozy and warm. Oh, Talon, I love them!"

"Alright, do the other'n."

She opened the rectangular package and was thrilled to find a matched set of brush, comb and mirror with filigreed silver on the handles and back. "Oooohhh, my! These are beautiful! Where on earth did you find them?"

"Apparently some pilgrims on a wagon train needed supplies more'n they needed a mirror so they traded 'em off at that Bijou Creek station," he explained.

Ginny sat her new treasures down on the table and walked into the bedroom and returned with a package behind her. She smiled as she handed it to her husband who was just as surprised as she had been. She nodded at him to open it and he pulled at the string and packaging and revealed a new knitted scarf and socks. And under them was a pair of fur lined elk-hide mittens with long roomy cuffs. He grinned as he put his hands into the mittens and said, "Boy, these sure woulda been nice to have on this last trip."

Ginny went to him and grabbed the other mitten and showed him how they were made with a special flap that covered an opening he could use for his trigger finger. He was very pleased with his gifts and knew she made everything with love and thinking only of his needs. He was filled with a special appreciation and love for this new wife that he truly felt was a gift from God. He felt a tear starting and he cleared his throat and said, "Well, you women had better get to busy with dinner while me'n Johnny go get you some more firewood."

When they returned, each partially hidden under a pile of firewood in their arms, they savored the aroma of the two turkeys on the iron spit over the hot coals in the fireplace. A Dutch oven hung from one iron arm that held the pot suspended over the edge of the hot coals. Another Dutch oven sat at the edge of the coals with more coals heaped atop it. The women were seated at the table as they watched over their handiwork. The men had no sooner dropped their firewood when a knock at the door surprised them, but Talon knew it would be Bull and he quickly stepped to the door to let his friend enter.

"So, Bull," started Ginny as they sat at the table, having finished their desert of apple pie, "your last trip, exciting wasn't it?"

Bull recognized a trap when he saw one so he glanced at Talon and caught his stern look. He turned back to Ginny and said, "Exciting, no, cold, yes. That wind outta the northeast is the coldest thar is an' we was glad to get to the station an' warm up, yessir we was."

Ginny had caught the exchanged looks and said, "Oh you two, trying to get anything out of either one is like pulling teeth."

Mary Sue piped in and said, "Now Ginny, whenever a man doesn't tell you all the details it's usually because he's either protecting you or he doesn't think they're important. Either way, you just have to accept it, because you're certainly not going to change them. At least that's what my Momma always said."

Talon looked around the table at his friends and his wife and smiled as he thought, *I'm certainly a lucky man. A wonderful wife, good friends, a good home, yup. I'm blessed of the Lord.*

To The Overland Trail

Chapter Twenty

Julesburg

THE BLACK OF NIGHT stubbornly resisted the approach of the grey of early morning but as it gave way the mass of mounted Indians stood as silent as a painting. Big Crow, the chosen leader of the assembled Cheyenne, Arapaho and Lakota, kneed his horse forward and with hand signals chose ten warriors. He pointed out Black Wolf and quietly told him of the plan. With a nod and a motion to the other warriors, Black Wolf reined his horse to the dip of a saddle between the two low bluffs that now obscured the massive band of over 1000 warriors, painted and ready for war.

Black Wolf led his men slowly toward the towering 18-foot sod walls of Fort Rankin. They lay along the necks of their horses and whispered to them as the mounts walked silently across the dusty prairie. When they were within 100 yards of the fort, the rising sun dropped its brilliant rays of morning to light the fort and they heard the shouted alarm. Instantly they rose up and shouted their war cries and goaded their horses into an all-out charging run toward the open gates of the fort.

The sentries quickly pushed the massive gates shut and dropped the bar to lock it tight. The other soldiers were caught sleeping but were quickly roused from their bunks with the combined noise of shots from the sentries, the blast of the bugle sounding reveille quickly followed by assembly, and the screams of the charging Cheyenne. Grabbing at their boots and shirts, the men crowded each other at the door as they snatched their rifles with one hand and slipped their suspenders over their shoulders with the other. Most had dropped their shirts in favor of their caps and hats as they stumbled to the walkway near the top of the sod walls.

Captain Nicholas J. O'Brien staggered from his quarters strapping his pistol belt around his middle. He ran across the parade grounds to the stairs to the walkway. His heart pounding in his chest and sucking air, he peered over the wall to see about a dozen mounted Indians screaming and taunting the soldiers as they rode their horses around the massive walls, dropping to the off-side of their mounts whenever they saw a soldier placing his rifle on the wall to shoot. The rattle of the staggered shooting from the walls broke the captain's concentration but he soon realized the small number of attackers and he turned to Sergeant Major Hunnicutt who stood at his elbow and ordered, "I want four squads mounted and ready in five minutes! We'll take care of them cussed heathens!"

With a crisp salute, the grizzled war veteran answered, "Yessir!" and turned to summon the troops. He trotted along the walkway slapping every other trooper on the back and instructed them to "Mount up and be ready to move out in five!" By the time the Sergeant Major finished his trot around the walkway, he took the steps two at a time and strode across the parade ground, motioning to any other troops and shouted the same instructions to them. Within moments, two rows of troopers were standing in front of their horses, waiting for orders.

The Captain, followed by the bugler, Jeffrey Richards, rode to the front of the assembly. Sergeant Major Hunnicut barked, "Ah-ten-shun!" The men snapped their heels together, slapped their thighs with their hands and with chins tucked in and chests stuck out stood stiffly at Attention. "Mooouuuunnnt Up!" from the Sergeant Major brought the men quickly aboard their mounts, sitting stiffly and staring straight ahead with right arms straight at their sides and the reins held loosely in their left hands. At a nod from the Captain who turned his mount toward the gate, the Sergeant Major ordered, "By the twos, left wheel, Ho!" and turned his own mount to follow close behind the Captain. As they neared the gate, the order, "Rifles at the ready!" prompted the men to draw their rifles from the scabbards under their right legs and rest the fore-stock on their left arm with a firm grip on the pistol-grip of the stock. As the gates swung open the bugler sounded Charge and following the Captain's example, they dug spurs into their mounts that responded with a coordinated lunge and the chase was on.

When the Indians saw the gates opening, Black Wolf shouted his orders to the warriors to follow him and wheeled his mount around to flee from the pursuing troopers. The Cheyenne had about a seventy-yard lead as they dropped low on the necks of their horses and slapped their sides with their legs. With legs and blankets flopping and hair flying in the wind, the warriors perfectly executed their orders and led the troopers away from the fort.

Captain O'Brien watched as the Cheyenne fled and he laughed mockingly, "Just as I thought. When they have to face the cavalry, they turn tail and run!" Over his shoulder he shouted at Hunnicutt, "Look at 'em go, Sergeant!"

But the seasoned veteran of Indian fighting didn't respond but spurred his horse to move alongside the Captain. He shouted at the Captain, "It ain't like 'em, Captain. They might have friends waitin' over that rise yonder!"

"This is just a small war party, we'll get 'em and teach 'em a lesson to mess with the cavalry!" shouted the Captain in answer. He was eager for battle and wanted to show his men that these Indians were nothing compared to the might of the Cavalry. He believed Chivington was right when he killed every living Indian at Sand Creek, and even though he didn't get the glory that Captain O'Brien believed he deserved, he felt he could do him honor by following his example. He wanted blood, Indian blood, and he was determined to get it.

The horses were running as if in a stampede as the troopers bent low and grasped the pommel as the animals galloped in chase of the Indians. The dust from the attackers carried the fine grit to obscure the vision of the men, but the pursuit did not slack. Nearing the low saddle between the two hills, a shot and then two more quickly sounded.

Startled by the gunshots, the Captain hauled back on the reins and his mount dropped his butt and started a sliding stop that caused those behind him to either veer off or try to stop as well. He caught a glimpse of waiting Indians just over the rise in the direction of the gunshots and shouted to the bugler, "Sound Retreat!" and jerked his horse's head around to lead his men back to the fort.

The premature rifle shots came from a handful of young men out to prove themselves and this first taste of battle caused them to shoot too soon. Big Crow screamed his war cry and motioned to Spotted Tail, the leader of the Brule´ and Pawnee Killer, leader of the Oglala, to charge. When the tide of warriors crested the top of the low-lying hill, Captain O'Brien felt his heart stop and he hollered at the Sergeant Major, "We've got to make it to the fort!" stating the obvious.

The look on the face of the old veteran spoke volumes about his opinion of this green-horn captain. No longer in a stretched-out column, the troopers were in a horse race for their lives. But their mounts were winded and the fresh horses of the pursuing Indians soon caught up when the soldiers were about 300 yards from the fort. Captain O'Brien ordered them to "Circle up!" and dismounted. Now able to mount a defense, the men used their horses, both standing and prone, as shields and opened fire on the screaming Indians now circling the troopers.

At the first shots from the fort at first light, the people of the town fled their quarters and ran to the fort. While the Captain was chasing the decoys, the settlers made it safely inside the walls. Lieutenant Cooper had command and ordered the remaining troopers and about 40 civilians to take to the walls and be prepared to defend the fort.

Within moments, he saw the returning troopers and the pursuing horde of Indians and he ordered, "Ready at the wall! Hold fire until ordered!" He watched as the troopers drew nearer the fort, but when the Indians had overtaken them, the Lieutenant went to the cannoneers and ordered, "Fire to each side of the troops! One round each cannon, fire!"

The resulting explosions caused the Indians to back away and focus on the fort, giving Captain O'Brien and his men just enough time to make a run for the fort. Remounted, the Captain hollered, "Follow me men, back to the fort!" Some quickly swung aboard and spurred their mounts, others hung on to the saddles and were drug along, but fifteen would never ride again. One of those was the bugler, Jeffrey Richards, who lay with his bugle clutched in his hand but his eyes staring at the early morning sky with its dusting of pink in the East.

The Cheyenne warrior, Medicine Water, dropped from his mount and began to take scalps, the first being that of the bugler. The reins of the bugler's mount were still clutched in his other hand and the warrior jerked them away and quickly mounted his horse leading the bay gelding with the bugler's saddle and started for the town. Big Crow had divided his forces sending those led by Pawnee Killer and Spotted Tail to the town. The main purpose of this attack was to secure provisions for the increased number of people, Cheyenne, Arapaho and Sioux. Their task was to take all provisions from the town.

Two women led those with packhorses to load the goods that would be taken. Both women had proven themselves as warriors and were now given this responsibility to direct the other women and the keeping of the provisions.

Mo-Chi was to take charge of the captured horses and Coyote Howling would direct the women with the packhorses. Three young warriors were chosen to herd the stolen cattle.

Little Paw and Neva led the different bands under Pawnee Killer, while Red Hawk led a band under Spotted Tail to attack the town. They were surprised to find the town empty of its citizens but they didn't hesitate to run rampaging through the buildings and taking all the supplies. Barrels of flour, sugar and molasses were loaded into wagons taken from the livery. Sacks of beans and cornmeal were also loaded. Sides of bacon were tossed on top of the bags but unfamiliar with canned goods, they were ignored, until George Bent, the brother of William and half white/half Cheyenne grabbed a can, split it open with his knife and slurped down the oysters. The watching Cheyenne were not surprised at the action of their brother, but were disgusted by the contents of the can and chose to leave the rest of the canned goods behind.

Big Crow continued to direct the attack on the fort, but used the feinting action of his warriors only to keep the soldiers and others contained in the fort while the rest of his warriors sacked the town. By noon, a messenger from Spotted Tail told Big Crow the supplies were on their way back to their villages and the town was empty. Big Crow signaled his warriors and they left the fort and the town to return to their encampment South of the Republican river. They had only lost three warriors while the whites had lost fifteen soldiers and five settlers. Big Crow was happy with the battle and the taken plunder.

Captain O'Brien, now on the wall with Lieutenant Cooper, watched as the horde of Indians rode off to the South. He replaced his revolver in his holster and turned to find the

Sergeant Major only to realize he was one of the casualties whose bodies lay mutilated outside the fort walls.

Looking around he spotted Sergeant O'Reilly and shouted his order, "Sergeant! Get a detail and retrieve those bodies," as he motioned beyond the wall, "and prepare them for burial." The sergeant stepped to his duties as he hollered out the names of the 'volunteers' that were chosen to join him for the grisly task. Captain O'Brien descended the steps and started toward his quarters, then turned toward his office to fill out his reports.

He dropped into his chair behind the desk in the sparsely furnished office and grabbing a piece of paper, began to scribble out a message to his superior officer, General Robert Byington Mitchell, at Cottonwood Springs in Nebraska territory. *General Mitchell, Ft. Rankin attacked by 1000 hostiles thought to be Cheyenne, Arapaho and Sioux. 15 casualties, 5 civilian casualties. Town decimated. Request reinforcements. Captain O'Brien, commanding.* "Corporal!" he hollered for his clerk. A tow-headed young man stepped into the doorway with a, "Yessir."

"Get this to the telegraph and make sure it goes out right away," he said, waving the paper before him. The young man snatched the paper and turned to leave, stopped, turned around and saluted. When the salute had been casually returned, the young man left at a trot to the telegraph office. He ran into the open door and stopped at the counter, gasping for air and looked at the operator and waved the paper before him. When he caught his breath, he said, "The captain said this has to go out immediately!"

The operator, a civilian, looked at the young man and said, "Hold yore horses youngster. There ain't no telegram goin' out today or probly anytime soon. The lines are down an' I suspect it was them Injuns what done it. So, you can tell your captain there ain't no help a'comin', at least not by the telegraph."

The corporal ran back to the commandant's office and entered, saluted, and handing the message back to the Captain, said, "Sir, the telegrapher said the lines are down and there ain't any messages goin' out."

"Well then son, you better start prayin' those Indians don't come back anytime soon. They got us outnumbered ten to one and we won't have a chance against them the next time."

Chapter Twenty-One

Valley

THE TRAIL DROPPED OFF the bluffs and now followed the sharply defined but ancient banks of the South Platte River. The tall banks of clay had been sculpted by the run-off waters from the receding hills that rolled away like ocean waves to the South. Towers of sandstone and arches of soft stone stretched across the wind and water sculpted formations that, with a little imagination, took on the forms of ancient structures or bulbous figures of animals.

This area always fascinated Talon and reminded him of the stories heard at his mother's knee of distant lands of the Greeks and Romans and their magnificent temples and coliseums. The wheels of the coach plowed through the soft sand as the tired horses leaned into the traces, and except for the occasional jingle of the trace chains, their passing was silent. The grey cottonwoods, long dead and skinned of bark, stretched their skeletal fingers toward the distant sky yet stood as solemn sentinels over this stretch of wondrous road.

"Get that thar bullwhip ready, younker, these hyar tired horses need some encouragement to get up that steep hill yonder," instructed Bull, shaking Talon out of his reverie.

The Shotgun reached for his whip, coiled and hanging from the stock of his Henry, and prepared to do the bidding of the Jehu. They were looking forward to the night at Bijou Creek, although the accommodations were not the best, they figured the warm hay in the stable and their buffalo robes would suffice for a good night's rest. Although Bijou was rated as a 'Home Station' and had facilities for overnight stays and meals, it was the only home station that did not have a telegraph. The trip from LaPorte had been cold but uneventful and as always, the cold wind added to the misery and the men were tired. Word of the attack at Julesburg reached LaPorte after they left. It had taken more than a week for the telegraph to be fixed and the weather prevented the usual runs of the stage.

This was the first stage east since the first of the year and it was already the 13th of the month. Westbound stages still were not rolling and Bull and Talon expected their return trip would be the first. There had been rumors of Indian attacks on the outlying ranches, but nothing had been substantiated and those types of attacks had become commonplace. Talon and Bull were relieved when there were no sightings of Indians so far on this trip and they both looked forward to an undisturbed night of rest.

Bijou Creek station was manned by two men, Manuel Lopez and Moses Greene. Their duties were evenly divided, except for cooking which Moses, a freed slave from Mississippi, handled exclusively. A big man that hummed and sang constantly, Moses enjoyed his time before the stove, and those that partook of his offerings were made equally happy. This morning he had fresh and fluffy sourdough biscuits with his unique honey-butter generously slathered between the layers of goodness. He served up an omelet made from duck eggs and pork belly with sautéed cat-tail root.

Bull and Talon both asked for additional helpings which were given to the tune of 'Dine and Joe', *Ho, ho, ho! Don't go Joe, Stay along with Dinah, do Joe, do. The hoe cake's done, Don't go Joe. Go home in the morning.* His deep bass voice and cheerful spirit brought smiles to the coach crew and they downed the special breakfast happily.

The station sat back among the trees that lined the edge of the bluff overlooking the wide swoop of the South Platte and was shielded from the direct light of the morning sun that pushed its way above the Eastern horizon. It was time to get started on the next leg of their assigned journey. Depending on the weather and other conditions, they planned to make the 57 miles to Valley station to spend the night, then the fifty miles on to Julesburg the next day. That would put them into Julesburg on the 15th and with a one-day rest, they would start their return on the 17th.

The fresh team was a six-up of mules to cross the sandy road out of Bijou and start for Junction. Stops at Beaver Creek and Kelly's or American Ranch, then fifteen miles on to Valley for their next overnight stop. Bull and Talon pulled their buffalo robes around them and Bull slapped reins to move the coach out and on the trail. The fresh team seemed to be glad to be on the road again and eagerly leaned into their traces, rocking the coach on its way.

A muffled shout was heard from within the coach as one of the men, apparently the drummer, lost his seat and mumbled his disapproval of the driver as he sought to regain his seat with his back to the front of the coach. The other man was a surveyor for the railroad and chuckled at the discomfort of the portly drummer. Both men were bundled in heavy wool coats with mufflers and gloves and woolen headgear. Although protected from most of the wind, the cold still permeated the coach and traveling at this time of year was anything but comfortable.

The quick stop at Junction was done with no one moving from their seats and no conversation exchanged between the hostler and the Jehu except for, "Here's yore lines!" as the hostler passed the reins to Bull and received a grunt in return. The stretch of road between Junction and Beaver Creek rode the dips and hills and the only sign of life that was seen was a small herd of antelope that stared at the passersby without alarm.

While the hostler at Beaver Creek adjusted the harness of the leaders he said to Bull, "I'm surprised to see you fellas makin' this run, what with the goin's on at Julesburg."

"What's goin' on at Julesburg?" asked Bull as he watched the hostler.

"Why, that Injun raid, that's what. Ain't you heered 'bout that?"

"No, don't know nuthin' 'bout no attack. What was it, just another bunch on a raid?"

"No sir, from what I hear, near 'bout a 1000 o' them red devils hit the fort and the town. Killed a bunch o' them sojers, an' took everythin' the town had stored up fer winter. Looks like a bunch o' folks're gonna be considerable hungry for a while." The hostler didn't stop his fitting of the harness and stretching out the lines while he talked. He shook his head and said, "Wouldn't be surprised to see them Injuns hittin' all these stations soon enuff. After what ol' Chivington done, they ain't none too happy with the rest of us."

"When did this attack happen?" asked Bull.

"Oh, more'n a week back, I reckon."

"Why weren't we told about it?" snarled Bull, now angry at the news and what they were driving into.

"Telegraph's been down, from what they say. We only heerd 'bout it from one o' them fellers that works up at Kelly's ranch. They found out from somebody else ridin' through."

Bull slapped his leg and stomped toward the coach, mumbling to himself as he climbed aboard. Talon was already seated and bundled under his buffalo robe. Noticing the demeanor of his partner, he asked, "What's the matter Bull, that hostler say somethin' you didn't like?"

"You can say that. Did you hear 'bout the Injuns?"

"What about the Indians?" asked Talon as he came from under the robe and reached for his Henry.

"Not here, Julesburg. They hit the fort and town and killed a bunch o' folks and took all their supplies. A thousand of 'em."

"When?"

"Over a week ago."

"Why didn't they tell us?"

"Telegraph down," said Bull as he reached for the lines wrapped around the brake handle.

"That sure don't sound good. I take it we're still goin' on?"

"Yup, that what we do," replied Bull as he hollered to the mules, "Ándele!"

The reception at Kelly's was much the same, surprise the stage was running. The hostler added a few details to the attack on Julesburg but nothing overly alarming. With the team changed, trips to the privy made, and everyone aboard, the coach rocked away from the ranch station headed for their last stop of the day, Valley… fifteen miles to go. Godfrey's ranch was less than four miles from Kelly's but did not require a stop but as they rattled by, they saw the wall was now finished and a couple of the ranch hands waved as they passed. They were making good time and were growing anxious for the sight of Valley station.

A long dip between bluffs crossed a sandy creek bed in the bottom and as the team started the pull up the bluff, the coach slowed to a walk. Cresting the bluff afforded a view of the long valley that gave the station its name, but Bull leaned back on the lines and brought the coach to a stop.

Just over a mile below, Valley station was under attack by a band of Indians numbering about forty or more. Even at this distance, the screaming and shooting was as clear as if they were in the midst of the battle. Without hesitation Bull drew back on the lines to turn the coach around and the leaders sidestepped through the arch of a turn. Without his usual shout to start the team, the coach was soon on its way off the bluff and back on a return route toward Godfrey's ranch.

Once below the edge of the bluff, Bull slapped the mules and started them at a canter, hoping to make their escape without discovery. Talon dropped his robe at his feet in the boot as he turned around to unlimber his Spencer. The big gun had better far-range accuracy than the Henry, but only had seven rounds in its tube magazine. He turned completely around and with his knees on the seat, he faced rearward to watch for pursuit.

Bull said, "I'm gonna pull into Godfrey's and get a fresh team. We need to get as far away from here as possible and Godfrey needs to be told about the attack."

"Ain't nuthin' followin' us so far, so go 'head on."

When the ranch and its fortified walls came into view, Bull kicked the team up to a gallop and they raced through the gate dragging a cloud of dust with them. As he leaned back on the lines, Bull shouted, "I need a fresh team! Indians are attackin' Valley station!"

Old man Godfrey with his long white beard was watching from the veranda of his house but he heard Bull's shout and quickly came to the aid of the hostler that worked with the team. He hollered to Bull, "How many?"

"Looked to be at least 40, maybe more. Looked to me like them sojer boys were makin' some kind o' fort out of sacks of corn and away from the station. I think the station was already on fire so I don't know if their telegraph got the word out. But we ain't goin' into that mess. I ain't lookin' to lose my hair at my tender young age," stated Bull as he ran his fingers through his thinning hair.

"Young? You ain't too far behind me Bull an' my woman says I done outlived my usefulness," declared Godfrey. He looked up at the big man and said, "There ya' go! You better be puttin' some miles behind you if you don't want them Injuns catchin' up."

"That's exactly what I aim to do!" declared Bull as he pulled the leaders around to leave the compound. He knew they would be traveling in the dark, but last night had a full moon and tonight's should be just as big. He would do whatever he could so they could be free of Indians.

To The Overland Trail

Chapter Twenty-Two

Blood

TWO COWBOYS FROM THE Kelly Ranch, also known as the American ranch, walked their horses through the cottonwoods along the bank of the South Platte. Strapped behind their cantles, both men carried double bladed axes and one of the men, called Big Steve by the other occupants of the bunk house, dragged a sled behind his horse.

Gus Hall said, "So, Big Steve, it looks like there's plenty o' standin' dead wood up yonder. That oughter be 'nuff for a sled load o' firewood fer the boss, ya think?"

"Looks good 'nuff to me. If'n we drop a couple them snags, I'm thinkin' it'll make a load." They were looking at the cluster of grey standing dead cottonwood that marked the floodplain of the flats. Nearing the dead trees, they were startled by the sudden appearance of Indians coming from the thicker woods near the riverbank.

Steve dropped the rope towing the sled and hollered to his partner, "Make for the bank!" as he wheeled his horse toward the higher clay bank behind the downed trees and driftwood. The two men made the twenty yards to cover and were off their horses with rifles in hand as they scrambled for cover behind the driftwood pile. The Indians instantly gave chase and the air was filled with screams of war cries as the Arapaho, Heap of Buffalo, shouted orders to his warriors.

Both cowboys had new Henry rifles and opened fire on their attackers that scattered to find their own cover. There were close to 100 warriors in the group and Heap of Buffalo directed his men as some had already dismounted and sought cover behind the scattered debris on the sandy flats. He ordered Red Hawk to take a group back through the trees and up the bank to come at the two men from behind, others were to continue their assault directly at the two men.

With so many attackers, both Gus Hall and Big Steve looked at one another as Gus said, "I think we done bought it, partner," and fired at one of the attackers, missing.

"It's shore lookin' thataway," choked Steve as he grabbed at an arrow that was buried in his chest.

Gus looked back at his partner and said, "Steve! Hang in there, partner, maybe some help'll come from the ranch!"

The big man's hand dropped from the arrow and he looked at Gus and said, "We . . . we . . . had us some . . . good times, didn't we?" The whisper of an arrow caused Gus to turn back to face the attackers. He squeezed off another shot and answered Steve, "We sure did, Steve O, we sure did."

Gus watched as most of the Indians seemed to be leaving. There were still a few scattered behind the driftwood, but those still on horseback faded back into the trees, leaving the others behind. One stood, partially covered by a ragged stump, to launch another arrow but Gus's aim was true and the red blossom on the warrior's chest told the cowboy he scored a hit as the warrior's arrow fell short when the bowman crumpled in a pile beside the stump. *Yeah! That was for Steve!* thought Gus as he jacked another round into the chamber.

He leaned the Henry on the log and pulled his revolver to check the loads. He knew he was running short and didn't know how long he could hold out. He spun the cylinder of the revolver as an arrow caught at his sleeve and stuck in the log. Gus looked up just in time to see an Arapaho warrior notching another arrow and he fired his revolver, killing the man.

He spun back around and saw the others flee into the woods. Looking back toward the bank, there were no other attackers. He waited and watched, but they were gone.

He started to stand, but stumbled at a sharp pain in his ankle and fell forward. He looked at his boot, saw a hole, and looking further realized he had taken a bullet across his ankle. He looked around to find the horses gone, Steve dead, and he was wounded.

Now what am I gonna do? As he was thinking about his dire situation, distant gunfire told him the ranch was under attack.

Heap of Buffalo had instructed his warriors, one band under Red Hawk, one with Spotted Owl, to use the bluffs and take a position behind the ranch houses. At his signal, the combined forces launched their attack on the defenders of the American Ranch.

With over one hundred warriors attacking, the defenders, Bill Morris, his wife Sarah, two young boys and five cowboys, were soon overwhelmed. In the first attack, Heap of Buffalo ordered his men to launch fire arrows at the buildings which quickly caught fire forcing the defenders from their protection. All the men were quickly killed and as a warrior raised his tomahawk to kill Sarah, he was stopped by another warrior named White White, who claimed her for his own. The boys were also taken captive, but even as they left, one of the boys had his throat slit and was left alone among the sagebrush.

"Look yonder!" said Talon, his voice revealing concern and even fear. He pointed to the Southwest, the direction the road would take them and about the distance where Kelly's station lay. A tendril of grey smoke blew along the horizon and gave both men a sense of foreboding. Behind them was the ranch of Godfrey and beyond that the Valley station that had been attacked, but the smoke before them warned of another assault and more Indians. They couldn't turn back, and to go on would certainly take them into another conflict. Talon looked at the Jehu and asked, "Looks like we're twixt a rock an' a hard place... do we or don't we?"

Bull had slowed the pace of the team to a walk and considered their options, which were none. Where they were now afforded no cover other than the occasional swell of a bluff or the drop of a gulley, the flats were devoid of trees except those along the river bank and to take the coach closer to the water was dangerous with the deep sand that made it almost impossible to move the coach.

It was bad enough when the roadway held the loose sand but to try to move the coach along the flood plain was nearly impossible. When the South Platte overflowed its banks with spring runoff, the river that was usually 15 to 25-yards wide, spread out across the flats to a width of a hundred yards and more, bearing with it the fine sand brought with the floodwaters.

Two choices remained, continue southwest toward home, or turn around and try for Julesburg. "I think our best bet would be to keep goin' but take it easy. Mebbe we'll be lucky an' them redskins'll be gone by the time we get there."

"Well, one thing we know for sure, there's plenty of 'em behind us!" declared Talon.

As they neared the ranch, it was evident there was no one nearby. Even before they reached the remnants of the still smoldering buildings, they spotted scattered bodies. Talon said, "I'm gonna check on all them," motioning toward the bodies. He dropped from the box while the coach still moved to make his way toward the first body.

He was vigilant of his surroundings but quickly came to the side of the first body. It was a man, or appeared to be, his body had been scalped and mutilated beyond recognition, but his boots told Talon this was a cowboy. He continued to look for others, finding five more bodies, one boy and four more men.

The grey whiskers on one body told Talon this was Bill Morris. He also saw signs, pools of blood, where as many as three other bodies, probably Indian, had fallen but were now gone. He looked around at the devastation and trotted to the coach. The two passengers were standing beside the coach, speechless, while Bull walked forward to make a quick check of the mules.

"Six bodies; one boy, five men, no women," stated Talon somberly as he climbed back to the box. Bull joined him and leaned back around to ask the passengers, "Both you fellas aboard?" and was answered with a simple, "Yeah!"

Talon searched the horizon for any sign of danger, but saw none. Bull rocked the stage with his usual slap of the reins to start the team on its way.

To The Overland Trail

Chapter Twenty-Three

Chase

THE SETTING SUN WAS perched on the silhouette peak on the Western horizon. The wispy clouds stretched across the sky would soon be colored with the palette of the sun to bid its farewell for the day. The brightness of the distant orb was directly in the eyes of the big man with the lines in his meaty paws as he guided the long-eared and tired team pulling the coach toward the sunset.

Beaver Creek station was nestled in the trees on the edge of the bluff above the river, but as they approached they saw nothing but blackened ruins of the two log cabins and big barn that made up the station. Little tendrils of smoke still rose from some of the debris. As they approached, Talon searched the tree line and river bank for any sign of life but saw nothing. Bull also scanned the area with his head turning on the stump of a neck to search his surroundings. He started to lean back on the lines when Talon shouted, "Go! Go! Here they come!" as he pointed to the tree-line.

Bull slapped the reins and shouted "Ándele!" as he leaned forward and added, "Come on you lop-eared cayuses!" The mules were startled by the slap and shouts and leaned into their traces and dug deep in the dirt of the roadway. The coach rocked back and the passengers were thrown to the floor as the coach lurched forward.

Talon twisted in his seat and took quick aim and fired a round at the charging Indians as they screamed and fired a flurry of arrows. One buck was dropped from his horse as Talon's Spencer scored a hit. He jacked another round, cocked the hammer and took aim again. With the rocking of the coach, the bullet flew wide of its mark but the roar of the Spencer caused the slightest hesitation on the part of the attackers as they looked at one another, noting the fallen comrade. But they slapped the ribs of their mounts with their heels and gave chase after the retreating coach.

The quick action by Bull and the shooting of Talon gave the coach a lead of almost two hundred yards, but the only cover offered by the terrain was sagebrush and buffalo grass. Bull leaned into his work and continued to shout at the team as he slapped the lines on their rumps. The mules stretched out into a full gallop and began to lengthen their lead. The road rose over a slight bluff and dropped into a long valley. The coach and team were kicking up a cloud of dust that obscured their vision behind them, but their concern was what lay ahead of them.

With so many of the stations and ranches already destroyed, would they run into another bunch of attackers? Or would they escape this bunch? The mules pace began to slow and their heads were no longer held high. But they labored on and the rhythm of their hooves brought encouragement to the Jehu and the Shotgun. Talon repeatedly looked behind them as well as searching the surrounding terrain but there was nothing.

"Hey, maybe we can slow it a bit, give the team a breather, I don't see any Indians anywhere," shouted Talon to his driver.

Bull turned to look at his Shotgun partner, leaned back and let the mules slow their pace. He let them drop to a walk. With the slower pace, the dust cloud settled behind them. The sun had dropped below the horizon and the resulting colors of the sunset spread across the sky to reflect on the entire countryside around them. But they couldn't bask in the beauty of nature, they were in trouble, Indian trouble.

After just a few moments of walking, Bull noticed the mules' sides were no longer heaving and they were breathing easier. The short breather had served its purpose. As he started to lift the lines, Talon said, "Here they come! I think they've got blood in their eyes!"

Again, the team lunged forward and the dust rose behind them. The roadway ran along the edge of the bluff above the Bijou Creek station and Talon stood up for a better look. Nothing remained but the same blackened timber. He slapped Bull on the back and hollered, "Keep goin'! Ain't nuthin' there!"

With the shadows of dusk, their visibility was fading, but Bull knew this part of the road well. With the Indians gaining on them, they couldn't slow down, but the road made a sharp turn and a steep drop off the bluff. Below the bluff, the road led to the Orchard station and maybe, just maybe, it was intact and they could stop or at least get a fresh team. The chill of the winter dusk came suddenly like a cold wind out of the North and the remnants of the last snowfall were blowing across the road. *I sure hope we can make this . . .* thought Bull as they approached the edge of the bluff.

He leaned back on the lines to slow the team just enough to make the sharp bend and as the leaders disappeared over the edge, he held his breath, hoping the sure-footed mules kept to the road. Instantly the coach crested the bluff and dropped over and around the bend as it chased the team.

Bull noticed a slight side slip with the coach and thought *Must be some ice, probably cuz of the shade from the bluff.* He leaned forward and encouraged the team, "Easy now, easy . . ." and he felt the coach twist with another slip. The roadway was narrow, the drop-off severe and if there was more ice . . .

149

the rear wheel dropped off the edge of the road and Bull felt the drop. He slapped the lines, but the wheelers, the team nearest the coach, hit a patch of ice and stumbled. The thoroughbraces of the coach squeaked at the strain and the front wheel beside the Shotgun also dropped over the edge. Bull continued to slap the lines and hollered at the mules, "Pull, blast it, pull!" but the coach was teetering on the edge. Then it began to tip and as Bull and Talon slid on the seat, Bull shouted, "Jump!"

Talon stretched up and out, Spencer in hand, and jumped into the shadowy darkness. Bull landed just below the edge of the road and was uninjured. He stood and saw the remnants of the coach scattered across the hillside. The dusk had quickly passed into darkness and he strained to see the bottom of the hill but could not. He was startled as several mounted Indians crested the bluff as they continued their chase. They reined up and Bull looked for cover, but there was none and he was unarmed.

The Indians shouted and kicked their horses down the roadway toward the big man. He frantically looked around, saw the broken whiffletree, grabbed it and waited for their charge. He roared at them, "Come on, you stinkin' Injuns! See what you can do against a real man!"

The Dog Soldiers drew rein and stopped to stare at the big man that taunted them. Black Wolf looked at Bull, kneed his horse forward a couple of steps, stopped and motioned to his warriors. Suddenly, eight arrows whispered past Black Wolf and pierced the massive chest of Bull.

He staggered back a step and said, "Why you, you . . . you kilt me."

He looked at the warriors who were notching more arrows, leaned back, sucked in a deep breath and yelled, "I'm Bull, Bull!" and roared like a mad grizzly, staggered one step, dropped the whiffletree, fell forward to roll down the hill, stopped against a large boulder, and died.

150

Talon saw nothing but heard the braying of the mules as they protested being pulled off their feet. The crashing of the coach on the rocky hillside was a clatter of metal against rock as the steel rims of the wheels hit rock. The coach was breaking up as it tumbled down the steep embankment. Talon hit first on his shoulder then the flat of his back.

The wind was knocked out of him and he caught a quick glimpse of the first stars of the darkening sky, then blackness as he felt he was smothered with a heavy weight. He tried to breathe, but air wasn't coming. He tried to lift his arms, but they wouldn't move. He tried to move his legs, but felt nothing. Struggling for breath, a slow-moving blackness crept from both sides, and he slipped into that blackness.

Three of the mules were dead, two were struggling with broken legs, and one stumbled down the hillside. The Dog Soldiers had no interest in the animals and after looking at the wreckage of the stage, as much as they could see in the darkness, they decided to leave.

Black Wolf motioned to his warriors and they mounted up, rode back up the roadway to the top of the bluff and looked back to see if there was anything to be seen. With no sign of life and nothing remaining that wasn't wrecked or destroyed, they left.

To The Overland Trail

Chapter Twenty-Four

Struggle

A THIN SHAFT OF LIGHT fought its way into the narrow opening to reach the face of the unconscious man. Shallow breaths whispered through his nostrils and life hung by a tenuous thread. A throbbing pain pounded from his leg to his mind to remind him he was still alive. Dust encrusted eyelids fluttered and finally one narrowly opened to see nothing but darkness.

He fought to suck air but realized he was hindered by a massive weight that covered his entire body. Alive but trapped, he tried to relax and think, remember why he was here, what had happened. And his thoughts flooded before him as he remembered the chase and the wreck of the coach and the encroaching darkness that hid everything and everyone.

But, where am I? He began to investigate and evaluate. *I can move,* he thought as he moved his arms and hands, however slightly. He tried his right leg and foot, felt movement and tried his left leg. *Uhnnnmm, must have hurt my leg pretty bad, maybe it's broke. Now, how am I gonna get outta here?*

153

He moved his left hand and began to scrape at the dirt beneath his hand and arm. Whatever was holding him down was heavy, but it wasn't rocks or dirt, *must be part of the stage.* Able to turn his head to the side, the bit of light coming in showed him he was right, it was the stage and it was the flat top that pinned him. He looked at the railing that was used to secure strapping and hold baggage on top and realized it was helping to keep some of the weight off him, but he was still pinned. *Well, I shore can't lift it off, I reckon I'll have to dig out from underneath it.*

He looked again at his left arm and hand and knew that was where he had to start and he began to use his arm and hand to start moving dirt. He cupped his hand and brought his arm down to his side in a sweeping arc, moved it up and brought more. It was cold, but he still had his buffalo coat and mittens on and was thankful. *Hopefully when the sun gets up, it'll warm things up a bit, cuz this is gonna take a while.* He knew he could freeze to death in this kind of cold, but maybe the exertion would keep his body heat up and he would be alright if he could dig himself out before he stiffened up with the cold.

The ground was hard from the frost, but fortunately this was sandy soil and since the moisture drained out easily it didn't freeze hard, not like moist soil that froze as hard as a rock and four to six feet deep in the cold winters of Colorado territory. *Well, whatever I did to my leg, at least the cold is keepin' it from hurtin' too much.*

As he scratched and scraped he tried to pull himself closer to the left so he could reach further and dig more. It wouldn't have to be a lot, just enough to squeeze out from under. He knew his body was not supporting the entire weight of the coach that it had to be resting on the rail and probably some rocks, but he still felt weight upon his chest and pelvis and thighs. *How am I gonna get out from under that weight? I've got to have something to pull on to get down into the dug-out area and get some relief.* He knew he had a lot of scratching before him and he continued, one sweep at a time.

As he mindlessly scraped and dug he thought. Remembering the attacks that brought him to this point he considered, *we saw Valley bein' attacked, but them soldiers were forting up behind those sacks of corn, but that means the station hands were done in, that'd be four, maybe six.*

And Kelly's, we found six but the woman and boy were gone so that's at least eight. Beaver Creek had another six and Bijou, Moses and Manuel. Let me see, that's at least 20 dead and that ain't even countin' those stations past Valley. Lemme see, there's three stations, Dennison's, Spring Hill and Antelope, and with at least four each, that's another twelve. Thirty-two dead! And that ain't countin' me n' Bull and them two pilgrims we were haulin'. Now it'd probably be my luck, I'd dig myself outta here and right into a passel of Indians!

He began to feel the cold in his toes, even though he had on a pair of those rabbit fur lined high top moccasins like he gave Ginny for Christmas, the lack of movement and other warmth was beginning to take its toll. He moved his feet as much as possible, but every time he tried moving his left foot, the pain in his lower leg caused restraint. But he moved anyway, knowing frostbite could take a terrible toll even to losing his toes and maybe even his feet.

He judged the time of day to be about mid-morning and he had been scratching and scraping since before full daylight. Slow progress, but progress nevertheless, and he continued. With more light, he was able to better assess his progress. He still couldn't move onto his side, just turn his head and he could feel the dirt give way under his shoulder and hip, but it would require a lot more.

He began to feel warm, maybe even sweat a mite, but he knew if he worked up too much of a sweat, it could freeze and the cold would permeate his body and do him in, so he began to think, *So, what do I do? I've got to keep digging or I'll never get out. Wait, maybe if I could shuck outta this buffler robe . . .* and he began to wiggle and squirm trying to undo the bone and loop fasteners with his left hand, then his right. Peeling the coat back away from his chest, he began to try to pull his arm back and out. He realized just getting out of the robe would give more room and maybe better movement. He squirmed and wiggled thinking of a snake shedding its skin. Finally, his left arm free, he slid his rump then his chest, just enough, to free his right arm and he realized he had slipped to his left and was now in part of his dug-out trough.

With more leeway to move and turn his head, he extended both arms straight over his head and tried to roll to his stomach. Twisting his body, he slowly but painfully rolled to his stomach. Now he could see his predicament better, but he also realized that without his coat, it was cold and the fingers of winter stretched under the coach to remind him just how cold.

Now he could pull the dirt back like a crab digging its den in the sand, and renewed by the progress, he dug fervently. As he dug, there were several river doney stones, those rounded by the current dragging them downstream, and it took greater effort to free them and remove them from his trough. Finally, thinking he had a large enough opening, he dragged himself forward.

It was a tight squeeze and for a moment he thought he might get stuck, but as soon as his head was out from under the coach top, he looked around as much as possible before pulling himself farther. His leg protested and he winced with the pain but reached for a large jagged boulder, and catching a handhold, he pulled. As he dragged himself free, he latched onto the robe and brought it out with him. He lay flat on the sand and soaked up the warmth as he fought to gain his breath and strength. A few moments later he pulled himself up to sit on the boulder and assess his predicament.

He carefully pulled up his pants leg and pushed the high-topped moccasin down to examine his injury. Just above the ankle, his leg bent to the side, *that's not good! Now, how am I gonna set that?* He knew it would have to be set soon and splinted before he could move much on it and before it started healing. If the bone started healing like that, he would be crippled for life. He looked around at the wreckage of the coach for anything he could use. As he looked up the hill at the strewn wreckage he spotted the twisted bodies of both passengers and knew immediately they were dead. From his vantage point, he could not see any sign of Bull, and if the big man survived, maybe he went for help or tried to escape the Indians. In any event, he couldn't count on anyone but himself.

He spotted the bodies of the mules and noticed the leads were still in the harnesses, they would be of use. He saw a couple of the single trees that were unbroken, one of the lap robes he and Bull had used, and scattered over the rocks and brush of the hillside were mail pouches and loose mail making it look like a snow storm of letters.

He slipped back into his buffalo coat as the breeze from the river assailed his tired body. Before attempting the scaling of the hillside to retrieve the leather reins and anything else, he needed to figure out where and how he could set the leg. *First, I need to set the leg, that's gonna hurt, then splint it and bind it up. Then I'll need to cut me a sapling for a crutch, wait, where's my rifles?*

He vaguely remembered clutching his Spencer while he was still under the coach and knew he could retrieve it, if it wasn't damaged that is, but where was the Henry? He turned and looked over the hillside for any sign of his rifle, then looked around the remains of the coach, and remembered it had been at Bull's side so both men would have a weapon against the Indians. Did he still have it or did he lose it when he jumped. *I better get my Spencer and then start on my leg. I'll look for the Henry later.*

To The Overland Trail

Chapter Twenty-Five

Challenges

TALON CRAWFISHED HIS way up the hillside toward the carcasses of the mules. He had fashioned a sling for his Spencer and it was held on his back as he dragged his injured leg over the stones and brush of the steep hillside. It would have been a challenge if both legs were good, but now every movement was painful and rigorous. What should have taken just moments, had now become a time consuming and arduous task.

His stomach reminded him there was another challenge he faced, food. But that could wait, it wasn't like he hadn't missed a meal or two before and he needed mobility before he could accomplish much of anything. To get that, he had to get his broken leg set and bound up so he could get around. Now, as long as the Indians stayed away, maybe he could make out.

As he reached the first carcass, he sat up to catch his breath. Looking around for anything else he might salvage, he spotted a big boot and leg that he instantly recognized as Bull's. He looked around for any sign of other life, then looking in Bull's direction he spoke loudly, "Bull, Bull! Hey

Bull!" There was no answer and no movement. Talon knew he had to check on his partner, if he was injured and unconscious, maybe he could help him. He rolled off the stone he sat on and crawled over to where the body of his friend lay. Talon saw the twisted body, lying on his back, with many stubs of arrows protruding from his chest. Indians usually retrieved any arrows from their victims, but these had all broken off and would be unusable. Talon saw the number of arrows it took to fell his friend and mused *You musta scared the daylights outta them for them to use you as a pincushion like that. Gonna miss you, Bull. I'd bury you, but I can't even stand up my own self, much less dig a hole big 'nuff for you.* He looked around to see if the Henry could be found but it was nowhere to be seen.

Talon turned away from his friend and returned to the carcasses of the mules to retrieve the lines and anything else that he could use. He was relieved the cold weather kept the carcasses from stinking, it would be intolerable during the heat of the summer. He didn't like to see any animal suffer and he knew these mules hadn't died right away, there were signs of struggle in the dirt beside them.

He crawled along the carcass, tugged the lines from underneath and slipped his Bowie from the sheath between his shoulders and cut the reins close to the bits. He retrieved four long lines and after sizing up the single trees, he knew he couldn't use them for either splints or crutches, so he left them.

As he worked on retrieving the lines, he continued thinking about setting the leg and had formulated a plan he hoped would work. Now back on the flats after descending the hillside, he crawled to a cluster of young cottonwoods. He knew he would need to fashion the makings of a splint and a crutch and have them available as soon as he set his leg and now searched for the needed saplings. There was an abundance of willows and he thought the larger willows would do for his splint and he set about cutting several to length and trimmed the little branch protrusions.

He looked back toward the cottonwood saplings and saw one about the size of his arm and taller than he was and with a fork at about the right height. His Bowie made short work of cutting it to fit and he looked at his handiwork and knew he was now ready to set to on the setting of the bone.

Near the base of the hillside he spotted an outcropping of stone that he had chosen for its overhang as a shelter. It had been used by someone before as was evidenced by the soot on the back wall and the underside of the overhang, made from old campfires. His plan required him to crawl atop the overhang and use the weight of a stone to straighten his leg. With the leather lines coiled and hanging from his shoulder, the willow splints tucked in his belt at his back, he began his climb.

As he crawled to the edge of the overhang, he pushed a stone about twice the size of his head, before him. When he was almost in position, he sat up and began to weave lengths of the reins in a basket weave pattern with lengths outstretched to the side. With a basket of leather woven to the size of about a foot across, he rolled the stone onto leather. He stretched his injured leg to the front and tied the ends of the straps to his ankle so two straps hung on either side of his foot.

As he looked at his handiwork, he held two looped straps, one in each hand, that were about eighteen inches longer than the straps from his ankle to the basket weave. He thought again about his plan to suspend the rock over the edge with his leg hanging straight down and the weight of the stone pulling on his ankle to straighten his leg. He visually examined his handiwork, nodded his head believing it was going to work and began scooting to the edge, pushing the leather basket and stone along as well.

He lay his knife at his side, and gripping the looped lines tightly, pushed the stone over the edge. It dropped suddenly and he almost lost his grip, and bent to the side to hold it fast. He slowly moved his left leg the last few inches, pushing it with his other leg and leaning away from the edge so he wouldn't tumble over and probably break a few more bones. With his leg in position, he slowly lowered the stone as it took up the short slack in the lines between his ankle and the stone. Instantly he felt the pain and knew he had to quickly get it done or the pain could cause him to black out.

He dropped the stone to its length and gritted his teeth as he tensed all the muscles in his body against the pain. He stifled a cry but it escaped with a "Yaaaaahhhhh!" as the full weight of the stone pulled on his ankle and straightened his leg. He felt the bone grate and thought he heard a pop and he was certain his leg was set. Still holding the loops, he leaned to look down at his leg and lifted the weight slightly. *Now, I hope this works!* he thought as he dropped one of the looped reins and the stone fell free of the basket. He fell back on the slab of the overhang and breathed heavily in relief.

He sat back up and carefully brought his injured leg up to apply the splints. He slipped one of the lines under his leg and four willow splints alongside. Slowly he wrapped his leg with the flat leather rein, encasing the splints and making a tight wrap. With his buckskins and moccasin top under the splint, the tight wrap rendered his ankle immobile and the leg secure. He was pleased with his work, but now had to crawl back down to secure his crutch that lay under the overhang. He shook his head at his failure to bring it with him, but was pleased with himself anyway.

His Spencer was undamaged but the haversack that held his extra ammunition was missing as was the Henry. He was also aware that the missing haversack held some pemmican that would taste quite good about now, but at least with the Spencer and his Remington revolver plus his tomahawk and Bowie knife, he could survive. Game was plentiful near the river, shelter was near at hand and there were other items he could retrieve from the wreckage, like a buffalo robe, that would help his survival efforts. With his sapling crutch under his arm, he began to explore his surroundings so he could prepare himself for any unplanned happening, like the return of Indians or another winter storm. He didn't anticipate trying to go too far with his bum leg, so he had to make the best of his situation where he was, and that meant he would need meat.

He looked skyward and realized dusk was making itself known and his light would soon be gone so he needed firewood more than anything else. Food could wait, but warmth for the night couldn't. There was ample dead wood available with the snags of cottonwoods and scattered driftwood, but gathering and carrying it with one arm proved challenging. When he had gathered what he thought would last the night, darkness had taken daylight captive to hold it till the morrow.

With the back wall of the overhang as a reflector, he started his fire with flint and steel using the thin inner bark as tinder. The small fire was shielded by the overhang and the wall of stone to the side, giving Talon an almost cavernlike shelter that now warmed with the small fire. He let the fire die down enough to move the coals nearer the wall and spread them out to warm the place for his robe. Adding more branches to the fire to make more coals, Talon bided his time to prepare a warm place for the night.

His thoughts wandered to Ginny. He knew the stage was not expected for at least a couple of days, maybe three. But if the telegraph had been up at any of the stations that were attacked, the word might have been passed to LaPorte and if so, she would find out soon enough. He didn't want her to worry, but he knew she would, but thankfully she had her friend, Mary Sue, to share her concerns with and he knew they would be praying for him.

When the stone slab of his sleeping spot had been warmed by the coals, he brushed the remains of the coals back toward the fire and spread out his buffalo robe and wrapped up in his buffalo coat and the robe, he curled up for the night.

Before drifting off to sleep, he prayed for his wife and friends, and for God's guidance in the days ahead. Days that would be challenging at best, and deadly at their worst.

To The Overland Trail

Chapter Twenty-Six

News

GINNY STOOD, HANDS on hips, on her porch as she watched the approaching wagon making its way up the long road to their cabin. She recognized Mary Sue as the driver shortly after the wagon rounded the bend at the bottom of the hill and was happy to know her friend was coming for a visit. It would be the first visit since Christmas and she had been feeling a bit lonely since Talon left almost a week ago. She leaned against the porch post as Mary Sue pulled up in front of the cabin and greeted her with, "Hi Mary Sue! It's good to see you, I was just thinkin' about making a trip into town, but thought I'd wait till closer to time for Talon to get back," she said as she stepped down from the porch to welcome her friend.

The smile on Mary Sue's face soon faded and Ginny noticed and asked, "What's the matter, something wrong?" as she held her hand over her eyes to shield them from the bright mid-day sun. Mary wrapped the reins around the brake handle and moved across the seat to step down. Once on the ground she turned to Ginny and said, "I'm afraid there's news, and it's not good."

"What is it? It's Talon isn't it, something's happened to him!" she said with a trembling voice.

"Now, we don't know that. Here, sit down, and I'll tell you everything I know," as she pointed to the two chairs on the porch. When they were seated, Mary began again, "The station got a telegram from down the line. There's been some Indian attacks on the stations."

"But what about Talon, tell me please," interrupted Ginny.

"We don't know, Ginny. The station keeper, Mr. Porter, said the telegram said many of the stations, mostly those closer to Julesburg, had been attacked and burned. But he had no word on the stage. He said the telegram came from Latham and the lines were down further on so they couldn't find out anything until the line's repaired."

"Well, how did the Latham station know, were they attacked too?"

"No, he said a rider from one of the ranches nearby gave them the word."

"Do they know if all the stations were attacked?"

"Ginny, I told you everything I know. When was Talon due back?" asked Mary Sue.

"He said he'd probably be back Saturday night if the weather wasn't too bad. Course that doesn't count for Indian attacks." She dropped her face to her hands and mumbled, "Oh God, he's got to be alright, he just has to, please God."

Mary Sue reached for her friend's hand and squeezed it as she said, "Ginny, we know Talon's in God's hands and God has done a pretty good job of takin' care of that man, so we need to trust Him now."

"I know, Mary Sue, but I can't just sit around and pray all day. Let's go back into town, I want to talk to Mr. Porter and see what he has to say. Maybe he's found out something more." She rose and pulled at Mary's hand to get her friend to take her to town. Mary stood and nodded her head, knowing any argument would fall on deaf ears, and walked to the wagon.

"I want to know about my Talon! Where is he?" Ginny demanded as she entered the station. Henry Porter raised his hands in a defensive posture and answered, "Now, Miss Ginny, we really don't know nothin'!"

"Did you get any other telegrams about the Indian attacks?" she asked as she stood with hands on the counter.

"Look, all we know is there were several stations attacked and burned. We don't even know which ones and how bad the damage is and we won't know till we send somebody out."

"When are you sending someone out?"

"I dunno, we sent word to Camp Colllins, but most of them soldier boys were sent up North to Fort Halleck and won't be back for some time, if ever."

"Isn't there somebody else? Somebody from the stage line?"

"No m'am, all we have on the payroll are drivers, shotguns, and messengers. Other than the hostlers and such at the stations, that is. There really isn't anybody else."

"Well, we can't just sit around and do nothing!"

"Now, Miss Ginny, the stage isn't even due back until tomorrow night, and we'll get a wire when they hit Latham, so we don't even know if there's anything that's happened."

"What about the other stations, where's the next telegraph?"

"Between here and Julesburg, there's just Latham and Valley. But the line's down and we don't know where, so we can't even reach Valley or Julesburg."

"Something's wrong, I can feel it, I just know it, and Talon needs help. Isn't there anybody?"

"Like I said, Miss Ginny, we don't really know if there's anything wrong and no, there's nobody I can send. And even if I could, I'm not too sure it would be the right thing to do what with all them Indians doin' what they're doin'."

"Ohhhhh, something's gotta be done, even if I have to do it myself!" declared Ginny as she turned to leave. "Come on Mary Sue, take me back to the cabin."

Ginny fidgeted and fussed all the way back to the cabin, but as they pulled up out front, she said to Mary Sue, "Might as well come on in and have a bite to eat. We missed lunch, but we still need to eat."

The two women stepped down from the wagon and Mary Sue slipped the reins around the hitchrack to tether the horse. Inside, Ginny put a pot of water on the stove to make coffee and started slicing some thin slices off the roast from the night before. Mary Sue picked up the plate with a loaf of sourdough bread and placed it on the table. When she was seated, Mary Sue started slicing the bread while Ginny put the coffee grounds in the pot, she had taken to using a cheesecloth bag to contain the grounds and dropped the bag in the water.

Ginny was unusually quiet as the friends dined on the roast beef sandwiches and coffee and Mary Sue suspected her friend was planning something. "So, what are you up to?" she asked.

Ginny looked up at her friend and feigned surprise, "What do you mean? I'm just eating my lunch."

"Oh, come on, Ginny. I know you and I know you're up to something. What are you gonna do?"

"What can I do, Mary Sue? There's nobody to send out, no way of finding out, and Indians all about, what can I do?"

"Well, we can pray, can't we?"

"Oh, I've already been doin' that, and I'll keep doin' that, but you're better at that than I am, so I'm countin' on you to keep prayin'," she said somberly.

"Well, I'll come up and see you every day and we can pray together, how would that be?"

"I'll be okay, you can check on me occasionally, but maybe he'll be back soon and everything will be alright. We'll pray that way, okay?" asked Ginny.

"Do you want me to stay here with you tonight?" asked Mary Sue.

"No, no, you go ahead on and get back to town before it gets dark. I don't want to have to be worryin' about you too," assured Ginny, forcing a smile.

She stood leaning on the porch post as she watched her friend drive her wagon down the long road back to town. With the sun still cradled on the mountains behind her, she knew her friend would be back at the hotel well before dark.

As Mary Sue disappeared around the bluff, Ginny turned back to the cabin and began to consider what she believed she must do. If she proceeded with her preliminary plan, there was a lot to do and she began to calculate all she would need and what she must do, crazy though it seemed, she knew she must and any further deliberations would be a waste of time.

She felt she had no choice, if she lost Talon, she knew she would have no reason to live so she couldn't lose him, she just couldn't.

To The Overland Trail

Chapter Twenty-Seven

Alone

GINNY SAT DOWN AT THE table with a hot cup of coffee before her and began to consider all she would need. As she thought about what she was planning she began to have doubts, but shook her head to still the questions and fear and replace them with plans. She began to list mentally what she would need. Realizing she would need the parfleche and saddle bags from the tack shed, she rose and went to retrieve them. She looked at the saddles and remembered the last time she and Talon rode the horses on their fall hunts and smiled at the memory. Brushing away a tear as she touched the seat of his saddle, and swallowed and set her chin and carried the bags and parfleche back to the cabin.

She sat the bags on the table and the parfleche on the chair and began to assemble her supplies. Wrapping the left-over roast and the sourdough bread, she dropped them into the parfleche. A wooden box on the counter held some of their smoked meats and she wrapped them in a piece of cloth and lay them in the parfleche. Coffee, sugar, beans, coffee pot and pan, salt, and cornmeal joined the other supplies.

171

Remembering the supplies in the root cellar, she went outside and into the cellar for some more cured elk meat and a handful of potatoes. The parfleche was now full and she sat it by the door.

The saddle bags were for ammunition, some strips of cloth for bandages, if needed, a tin of ointment, his mother's special recipe made from bear grease and who knows what else, another shirt and britches for her and another shirt for Talon. His revolver needed powder and shot, which she retrieved, hers required the paper cartridges and caps which were already in the bags. She also gathered more ammunition for her Henry and his Spencer. She knew she was probably forgetting something important, but hopefully she'd remember what it was before she left in the morning. She put the saddle bags by the door with the parfleche and gathered her heavy woolen Hudson's Bay coat, mittens and fur lined moccasins and put them by the door next to her Henry.

Believing she was ready, she went to the bedroom to try to get some rest. She knelt down beside her bed and began, "Lord, you know I need you, we need you, because I don't know what tomorrow's gonna bring. If Talon's in trouble, help him and protect him. And as I go to bring him home, protect me. Apparently, there's a lot of Indian trouble and you know I'm a bit scared of them because of what happened last time and I sure don't want to be taken by 'em again, so Lord, please watch over me and keep me from doin' sumpin' stupid. And I can't do this without you, so I'm counting on you, Lord. Don't let me down. Amen." She climbed into bed and rolled up in the covers and tried to go to sleep.

It was early morning, before first light, when she rolled out of bed and started getting dressed. She slipped her buckskin trousers on over the one piece faded red union suit, dropped the buckskin tunic over her head pushing her arms into the sleeves and sat on the edge of the bed to don her fur lined high topped moccasins. She wrapped her knit wool scarf around her neck, pulled the matching knit cap down over her ears and went to the door, grabbing her wool coat. She knew she would be in for some cold weather, maybe even snow, and she wanted to be prepared.

She saddled Talon's Grulla mustang gelding first, planning to use his horse as a pack horse until she found him. Then, after rigging her own sorrel, she led them both to the cabin. There was just a sliver of grey peeking over the flats to the East, but it was enough for her to do what she needed. Tethering the mounts at the hitchrail, she went back into the house and started bringing out the supplies. She strapped the parfleche into the seat of Talon's saddle, tied on the saddle bags behind the cantle and went back for their bedrolls. After securing the bedrolls behind each saddle and the additional supplies in the second set of saddle bags behind her cantle, she went back into the cabin.

Ginny sat at the table and began to write a note to Mary Sue. The stub of a pencil moved with her thoughts. *Mary Sue, when you get this, I'll be long gone. I'm going after Talon, I have to Mary Sue, you know I do. Please pray for us both and I'm sure we'll see you soon. You're my best and only friend, don't forget that! I love you. Ginny.* She put the note in the middle of the table, used the extra coffee cup for a weight to keep it in place, rose and looked around, then walked out the door.

Standing on the porch, she fastened her coat, pulled on her mittens, took a deep breath and mounted up. She whistled for Smokey and patted the rump of her horse and caught him as he leapt from the porch to the horse. She stroked his fur and said, "Now, you ride easy boy, we got a long way to go and a man to find. It's gonna take both of us, so let's get it done, boy." She dug her heels into the ribs of Red, her sorrel mare, and started off into the rising sun.

Her floppy felt hat was loose enough to cover her knit cap and she pulled it down to shield her eyes from the brightness of the rising sun. She had determined to follow the stage line road, at least to Latham and after that she would stay close to the road, if it appeared safe, otherwise she would ride closer to the river bank between the road and the river where there would be better cover.

The road seemed abandoned for the first part of the morning, and she found a likely spot for her lunch break. She knew she would have to be conscious of the needs of the horses for feed and water and found a small clearing among the riverbank of cottonwoods. She loosened the cinches on both saddles and tethered the horses on a long line to give them enough room for grazing on the growth in the clearing.

Stretched out in the shade of a small cottonwood, she munched on some smoked meat, tossed a piece to Smokey, and ate a left-over corn-meal biscuit. A big swig of water and she was ready to go, but knew she had to let the horses eat and rest a while before taking out again. She enjoyed the solitude and the cool breeze from the river. The water level was low but the water was clear. There was ice along the edge of the water and hung from some willows that arched over the bank, catching the splashing water as it rushed past.

Across the river, she watched a couple of otters playing in a snowdrift that was caught in a ravine and led to the water's edge. She laughed at their antics and enjoyed the brief respite from her worries. She stood and gathered the tether line and pulled the horses toward her. Tightening the cinches, she mounted up, whistled for Smokey, and started on the trail.

Mid-afternoon saw her on the roadway as it rose from a long dip between two low rising hills. As she crested the hill, she met two riders going West. They reined up as she neared and rested their hands on their pommels and waited. As she drew alongside the two, she kept her head down enough so the brim of her hat partially obscured her face and she knew her scarf was up around her neck and covered the lower part of her face. She was greeted by the two riders, who looked to be cowboys fresh off the range, with a "Howdy, friend. Goin' far?"

Her muffled voice came from under the scarf as she answered, "Just up to Latham, meetin' a friend."

"Have ya heered 'bout the Injuns?"

"Yup, but they ain't come this far yet," she answered.

"All right then, God speed an' keep yore topknot on!"

"You too!" she answered as she kneed her mount forward. She listened and heard the clatter of hooves as the men continued on their way. She was relieved to hear the "Godspeed" from the one for she feared for her safety, knowing that anyone traveling alone could meet trouble at any time.

Most often, western men were respectful of women and would defend them at any given time, but there was always the exception, especially if there was no one around to witness or hinder an attack. She was determined to maintain her ruse of being a man as she absentmindedly slipped her hand into her coat to feel the butt of her Colt Army pistol. It was loaded with six .44 caliber slugs and it was deadly. Its presence was comforting and reassuring.

She had proven herself capable under the tutelage of her husband but she also knew there were no guarantees, no matter how many weapons she carried. She knew the greatest danger she faced was the marauding Indians, they would have no mercy on a woman. But she couldn't let that stop her, she knew she would be facing danger of all kinds, but the safety and return of her man was all that mattered and she couldn't think about anything else.

To The Overland Trail

Chapter Twenty-Eight

Wicked

GUS HALL PUT THE HEEL of one boot to the toe of the other and pushed to remove the bloody boot. He knew he had taken a bullet but he had to see how bad the wound was before he could do anything else. With the boot removed, he examined his lower leg, wiping the blood with his handkerchief and by pushing down his woolen sock, saw the wound that cut his flesh, nicked the bone and brought a lot of blood.

He knew walking would be difficult, but he had to get away from this place. Wrapping his ankle with his handkerchief, he struggled to replace his boot and with considerable pain, the boot slipped back on. He wiggled his toes and felt the squish of his bloody sock. *Well, that was dumb. I didn't think to pour the blood outta muh boot.*

The cowboy climbed to the top of the clay bank to try to see what was happening at the Kelly or the American ranch. He had heard quite a bit of gunfire, but it had abated and he thought the fight was over. *Sure hope the Morris' are O.K., they're good people.*

When he crested the bank, all that was visible was a cloud of smoke from the buildings and he knew there would be nothing left. There were just too many Indians in the band that had attacked Big Steve and him and he knew from the smoke, the band of marauders were having their way. He shook his head as he thought of Sarah Morris and the boys, he didn't want to think what the Indians would do with them.

Gus took to the tree line and started downstream. He knew the Godfrey's ranch was the nearest, and the Wisconsin ranch was farther away from the river and further onto the flats. Maybe he could find help at one of those. His walking was hindered by the increasing pain in his ankle and he knew he was still losing blood. He looked behind him and saw each of his boot prints from that foot also had a spot of blood. It was getting late in the day and although closer, he knew he still had maybe a mile or more before he could reach the Godfrey's but he was worn out and didn't think he could walk another ten yards. Dark was coming and he was tired as he searched for some place to get some rest.

The sound of distant gunfire woke Gus with a start. He sat up, momentarily forgetting where he was, and looking around for the source of the gunfire, realized he had fallen asleep lying against a downed cottonwood. The grey trunk beside him gave shelter and even some warmth, but when he finally got his wits about him and realized where he was, he struggled to his feet and started downstream. He was fearful the gunfire was coming from the Godfrey ranch and as much as there was, he knew the ranch was under attack by Indians.

Roman Nose sat astride his horse with the butt of his rifle resting on his hip. He looked at the assembled band of Lakota and Cheyenne before him, nodded to Red Hawk on his left and to Spotted Crow on his right. Crow reined his mount around and motioned for his band of forty warriors to follow. His assignment was to circle behind the ranch with the walls and at the given signal, lob fire arrows at the buildings.

Roman Nose watched as the first band disappeared around the bluff and nodded toward Red Hawk. The second band of over thirty warriors moved away to their designated point of attack. After allowing time for the two bands to get in place, the war leader of the Cheyenne lifted his rifle and shouted his war cry. His band was the largest group of over seventy warriors and they surged forward shouting their war cries and attacking the Godfrey ranch.

Inside the walls of the ranch, Holon Godfrey and his wife Mildred, had just finished their breakfast when the shouted alarm came from one of his three ranch hands. Holon jumped to his feet, knocking over his chair and ran for the door, grabbing his Spencer on the way. He thought, *This is it! This is why I built that wall, now we fight!*

The newly built adobe walls surrounded the compound of the house, bunkhouse, grain-bin and root cellar. Just outside the walls, the barn and corrals stood unprotected. He saw the horde of attackers as they charged along the road towards the main gate of his walls, they were spread out and attacking en masse. Godfrey ordered his men, "Fire! Thar's so many of 'em ya cain't miss!" His big Spencer boomed and a charging warrior was knocked from his horse, to be trampled by those behind him.

As he jacked another round into his Spencer, he saw his wife poke her Spencer through one of the firing ports of the wall and echo his. Her shot was also true, even as it rocked her back and she fell to her back with her skirt and petticoats flying. Both laughed as Holon reached down to help her up, as his three ranch hands fired into the charging mob. The screams of the attackers, the roar of the gunfire from attacker and defender alike, and the resulting smoke from the guns fueled the battle.

When Holon helped his wife up, he saw the flaming arrows arching over the wall and striking the buildings. He hollered at one of his hands, "Shorty! Shorty! Get some water on them arrers!" as he motioned toward the buildings. They had placed several buckets of water around the buildings in anticipation of that type of attack. The day before they had watched the smoke cloud from their neighbors, at the American ranch and knew if they were attacked, the Indians would try the same thing.

The band under Red Hawk swept down on the corrals and loosed the horses, driving them away. As they left, they set fire to the grass and the barn, which caught the attention of Holon and he told his wife, "Keep 'em firin', you too! I'm goin' to take care o' that!" he motioned toward the fire at the barn.

He grabbed a bucket of water and with bucket in one hand and his rifle in the other, he went through the small gate in the wall and started for his barn. A scream from a charging Cheyenne caused him to drop to one knee, put the bucket on the ground, and as casually as if he was out for a stroll, he shot the warrior through the chest, dropping him instantly. He jacked another round, picked up the bucket and with about half the water, doused the beginning flames at the barn. Protected by the smoke from the barn and grass, he quickly walked along the fire line and doused the flames at the grass and ran back to the wall.

More flaming arrows arched over and struck the bunk house and grain bin. Shorty doused the bunk house, but didn't get to the grain bin in time to save it. He returned to the wall during a lull in the attack and reported to Holon, "Couldn't save the grain bin, but ever'thin' else seems to be alright."

Holon nodded his head in approval and turned back to watch the next attack. Roman Nose had groups of twenty warriors stagger their attacks as they pushed toward the walls. His goal was to completely destroy this ranch and kill everyone inside. But the walls with their firing ports offered few targets and the attacks were repeatedly repelled. Yet every attack saw warriors fall under the deadly fire from those inside.

After repeated assaults, and numerous casualties, Roman Nose was frustrated and angry. He led attack after attack and was repelled each time. Finally, he ordered his warriors away.

He looked back at the walls and raised his fist and in the language of his people shouted, "That is a place of death! The old man there will now be known as Old Wicked for the death he has dealt!"

Holon turned to Shorty and asked, "You know their lingo, what'd he say?"

"He said you were Old Wicked!"

"Whoooeee! You bet yore britches I am! We done it boys, we whupped 'em."

He turned back to the wall and peered out his firing port and looked at the scattered bodies of the attackers. As he watched the warriors leave, he opened the main gate and walked out to survey the damage done. He counted eighteen bodies of the attacking force and as he walked among them, he shook his head. *Even though they's Injuns and they wanted to kill us all, death is never a purty sight.*

As he walked back through the gate, he looked up and grinned, then he looked at his wife Mildred, standing by the three ranch hands, and announced, "We're gonna put us up a sign, right up thar," and motioned over the top of the main gate, "and we're gonna call this place Fort Wicked!"

Mildred shook her head and grinned at her husband with his scraggly beard and broad grin and said, "Oh, you men, you're all alike! Gotta be braggin' 'bout sumpin'."

To The Overland Trail

Chapter Twenty-Nine

Hunt

TALON'S FIRST THOUGHT as he woke was of food. The last meal he had was when Moses had fixed the duck egg omelet before they left Bijou Creek station early yesterday and with everything that happened his body had used up all his excess energy and was now craving a re-fueling. First light would be a good time to find a deer or antelope coming to the river for water and he rolled out of his buffalo robe anxious to find some fresh meat.

He bumped his leg against the back wall and grimaced with the pain, a reminder of his temporary infirmity. He knew he would be hindered in his hunt and was more determined to make it successful. He slowly stood and slipped the crutch under his left arm thinking he might need to find something to use as a pad or the crutch would soon rub him raw.

The overhang provided good shelter, but he couldn't stand to his full height without cracking his head on the overhead stone. Hunched over, he hobbled a couple of steps nearer the edge, paused to check his surroundings by the dim early light. Seeing nothing alarming, he headed for the cluster of trees nearer the river bank. On his earlier reconnoiter for firewood, he noted a game trail that wound through the cottonwoods to a cut in the riverbank where the animals could easily reach water's edge.

As he surveyed the area he spotted a cluster of alder and chokecherry and hobbled towards it. Looking back to the game trail, he believed he would have a good field of fire if he were prone in the bushes and dropped to his knees to make his way to a good position that hopefully would result in bagging meat.

He snaked his way back into the bushes so only the rifle barrel would be exposed. Using a nearby stone for a rest, he lined up his sights on a spot where an animal would likely walk from the trees to the water. On his belly on the cold ground, it didn't take long for the cold to permeate his body causing spasmodic shivers. He moved as much as he could to warm his extremities and get the blood flowing. As the morning light began to cast long shadows, he saw movement at the edge of the trees and watched.

Slowly, a big deer, a doe, tip-toed from the edge of the trees, her big ears pointed forward, listening. Her head moved side to side, neck stretched out as she sniffed for danger. A step, freeze and slowly observe, another step and wait. When her head moved to search the trees away from Talon, he slowly adjusted his position, waiting for the doe to move forward just a bit more to provide a better target. His hammer cocked and ready, he waited.

Another step, and suddenly as if she had springs for legs, she jumped up and crashed down to a heap, unmoving. Talon was startled, but didn't move. He saw the fletching of an arrow protruding from the neck of the doe and he watched as two Cheyenne walked from the trees to claim their prize.

Talon waited, unmoving and watching the two men as they field dressed the deer, all the while chattering over their kill. Shortly, the men hung the deer on a pole and carried off the carcass as it swung from the pole supported on their shoulders.

Talon waited a good quarter hour before leaving his lair under the brush.

He carefully and as quietly as possible worked his way through the cottonwoods toward his overhang. As he neared the edge of the trees, he saw the clearing crowded with Dog Soldiers, probably forty or more, gathered around a fire as they watched the hunters butchering the deer. Several had already speared their cut of meat with a green willow branch and hung the meat over the edge of the fire and now sat watching the juices drip on the coals and anticipating their meal.

Talon edged away from the tree line, ensuring he was behind the trees and that his movement, slow as it was, would not be seen by the band of Indians. As he leaned against the off-side of a big cottonwood, he looked for better cover. He spotted a downed tree with a lot of deadfall around it and a thick cluster of young saplings growing from the rotting wood. He dropped to his knees and slowly crawled to his chosen hideaway, careful not to make any sudden movements.

He knew, that even in the dark shadows of the forest one could remain unseen even if unprotected, if there was no movement. But Talon also knew he could not remain immobile and standing with his throbbing leg, so he chose to work his way to cover where he could take his weight off his bad leg.

As he crawled toward the downed tree, he had to wiggle through the cluster of young saplings and he was thankful they were without leaves, but they still moved slightly. Suddenly there was a shout from the band of marauders and Talon quickly rolled under the tree, reached out to the pile of leaves and small dead branches and covered himself under the debris. He slowed his breathing and waited.

Within moments, he felt rather than heard, the presence of someone and he could barely see through the pile of leaves a leg with fringed buckskins and beaded moccasins, tip-toe by his burrow. He purposely breathed shallow and unmoving, he waited. He heard the soft steps of moccasins returning to the fire and, understanding Arapaho from his childhood, he heard the man tell the others, "Probably just a fox or something, there's nothing there."

Talon breathed easier, but did not move from his lair, choosing to wait until they left. The breeze that whispered through the trees followed the river and moved from west to east. As the band of Arapaho and Cheyenne took their meal, they talked about the battles fought and those that were before them.

Talon strained to make out any of the conversation, a blend of Cheyenne and Arapaho. With his parents raised among the Arapaho, he learned the language, but not using it often, he found the mix of languages difficult to follow. What words he did pick up seemed to tell of their impending attack on the Orchard station for additional supplies and horses. Eagles's Nest did not seem to be a target, but they were bound for the Orchard station.

Talon tried to think of a way to warn the workers at that station, but he couldn't move from his hideout, much less hobble the four or five miles to the station. As he thought about them he pictured the men, the station keeper Davis and his wife, and the hostler, Cable. He knew this band of Dog Soldiers would show no mercy and kill all of them and burn the buildings, leaving nothing behind.

As he considered what they were about to do, Talon remembered what had been said about Chivington's massacre and knew if the tables were turned, he would probably be just as vengeful. But he felt the murder of women and children, whether by the soldiers or by the Indians, was something intolerable. He thought about how he would feel if someone murdered his wife, and if he had children that were also victims, he couldn't fathom how rancorous he would become.

As he pondered his situation and the events of the past few days, his mind was scrambled for direction and purpose. He needed to focus on getting home and if he had to hobble on his crutch all the way, then that's what he would do, anything to get home to Ginny.

With the Indians rampaging as they were, even a town like LaPorte could become a battleground. *I could sure use a horse about now, even a mule would do, anything that would help me cover some ground to get away. If I could rope a buffalo, I'd try to ride it!* He chuckled to himself as he pictured himself on a buffalo and squirmed under his leafy blanket. He froze as he heard movement, then realized it was the entire band preparing to leave.

When he was certain the Indians were gone, he slowly rolled from his bunker and struggled to his feet. He was still cautious as he approached the clearing until he was assured they were well away. Approaching the coals of the fire and the nearby carcass of the deer, he dropped to his knees to examine the remains for any possible meat. Just inside the front leg on the chest, he cut a thin layer of meat and using one of the willow branches, hung it over the still smoldering coals. He walked back toward the edge of trees and gathered an armful of firewood and returned to stoke up the fire sufficiently for his meat. As the first cut began to simmer, he continued to cut the scraps of meat left, mostly from the legs and neck. The smaller pieces he would smoke and save for a stew or something.

As he sunk his teeth into his first cut of meat, he sat back on the nearby log and savored his feast. As he ate, he thought about Ginny. *She's probably in town with Mary Sue and the two of them are dining on some fine meal, maybe a pork roast from one o' them farmers, prepared by Aunt Sophie. Hot coffee or tea, and they'll probably have some cinnamon apple pie for desert. Then she'll go home to a nice warm cabin and sleep in that soft bed under those warm blankets. Yup, she'll be so comfy, she won't even miss me. Oh well, at least she's safe and she'll stay that way, but she'll probably start worryin' soon if I don't get outta here.*

To The Overland Trail

Chapter Thirty

Cold

GINNY WALKED INTO THE Latham stage station and stepped up to the counter. With one elbow on the counter she looked at the man behind the roll-top desk and asked, "Have ya heard anymore 'bout the Indian attacks on the stations?"

The portly man with a friar's hairline that circled his head and rested on his oversized ears, turned to look at his questioner. "And just who might you be?"

"That shouldn't matter, but just so you'll know, I'm Talon Thompsett's wife. You know, he's the Shotgun on this run and we haven't heard from him."

The man stood up, pulled up on the garters on his sleeves, removed the visor from his brow and walked to the counter. "I'm sorry m'am, I didn't know. The last we heard was from a cowboy that came through. He'd seen the remains of the American Ranch and he shied away from the road after that. He saw smoke comin' from Beaver Creek and Bijou, but didn't check on 'em. Probably 'afeered he'd run into some o' them redskins."

"Nothin' else?"

"Nope. I figger the line's been cut, don't rightly know whereabouts, but cain't raise nobody cuz the line's deader'n a doorknob."

"All right then, thanks," she nodded at the keeper as she turned to leave.

It was late afternoon and she considered stopping at the nearby hotel for a meal but thought she would have a couple more hours of daylight and decided to put some more miles behind her. She swung aboard her sorrel, grabbed the lead on the grulla, and pointed them to the east on the stage line road. When she cleared the town, she began watching the tree line by the river for a possible camping sight and continued trudging along. Just as the sun dropped below the distant horizon, she saw a break in the trees that beckoned.

After tethering the horses near a few clumps of dry grass and within reach of water, she stretched out her bedroll near some chokecherry bushes. As she looked at her bedroll, she remembered Talon's example of using some pine boughs for bedding and to protect her from the cold from the ground. She looked around at all the cottonwood and the occasional elm and the many bushes, but didn't see anything resembling a pine.

Not wanting to have a fire for fear of giving away her location to any prowling Indians, she gathered several armloads of leaves, scattered them at the edge of the chokecherry, and repositioned her bedroll. She pulled the parfleche beside her and with a cut of the roast and the bread, had a cold, but satisfying supper before turning in for night. With her only companion, Smokey, her bedtime conversation was limited, but the two friends lay side by side and soon drifted off to sleep.

Twice during the night, she awoke shivering and adjusted her covers, and the second time she pulled the dog under the covers with her and slept better until the early morning hours when Smokey woke her with a low growl. With the dim light from the moon and stars, she clutched her Henry and watched as a black wolf trotted along the tree line searching for a meal.

As she watched, the wolf suddenly stopped and sniffed the air. He looked in the direction of the horses and hunching his shoulders and dropped into a stalking crouch and began moving toward the horses in a stealthy approach. Slightly obscured by the surrounding brush, Ginny whispered to Smokey, "Shhhh now, I see him, stay here boy, easy now."

She slowly sat up, bringing her rifle to her knee and taking aim at the black shadow some thirty yards away. Carefully lining up the brass blade sight between the buckhorn rear sights, she followed the slow movement of the determined wolf. His head slowly moving side to side to survey his surroundings, he froze in place as he looked in Ginny's direction.

The reflection of moonlight caused his eyes to appear as orange lights amidst the black fur and caused Ginny to tremble in fear. The big wolf hesitated and for a moment Ginny thought he was going to charge her. Smokey slowly rose to his feet, assuming a stance of attack and let a low rumble come from deep in his chest. Ginny knew the massive wolf would probably easily kill the smaller dog, but Smokey had the heart of a Grizz and knew no fear. The wolf took a tentative step in her direction and leaned his weight on his hind legs as if he was about to pounce when Ginny squeezed off her shot.

The roar of the Henry shattered the quiet night and the kick of the shot and the smoke from the muzzle temporarily caused Ginny to lose sight of her target but she quickly jacked another shell into the chamber and searched the night for the black monster. She had scored a hit, but though the animal had dropped, he struggled to get up and glared at Ginny as he bared his teeth and started to lunge for her but she fired again and stopped his charge.

The wolf's carcass fell less than fifteen feet in front of her and as quickly as it was stopped, Smokey leapt to attack. Within seconds he bit the neck of the big wolf and sinking his teeth deep in its throat, he shook his head side to side as he furiously growled. What life was left in the black beast was quickly extinguished as Smokey continued thrashing his head side to side.

Running to the side of her protective dog, Ginny, with another shell jacked into the chamber of her rifle, went to his side and placing her hand on his neck said, "Smokey, let go, he's dead. Good boy, good boy!" She dug her hand into the fur of his neck and pulled him back away from the carcass of the wolf, patted his head and continued her encouragement. "I think you'd have attacked that thing even if I hadn't shot him. But I sure am glad you waited cuz I'm thinkin' he'd of done you sumpin' awful!"

"So, Smokey, whaddayathink? Should we skin him out or not? I know if Talon was here he'd say we should, but I dunno if I wanna take the time." She looked at the eastern sky and saw the beginning of light chasing away the stars and said, "But if we don't, we'll probably wish we had. Maybe if we skin him out an' cache the hide, we won't spook the horses an' we can pick it up on our way back. Yeah, that's what we'll do. That all right with you boy?" she asked Smokey to be answered with his stump of a tail wagging so excitedly that his entire hindquarters shook. She grinned and set about her work with Smokey keeping watch.

By the time the full sun had finished painting the sky with the morning's colors, her Bowie knife had finished the task of skinning out the big wolf. Ginny was surprised at the suppleness and thickness of the fur and knew it would make a fine pelt. *Maybe I can even use this to line a nice coat. It sure would be a warm one!* she thought as she rolled up the hide tightly, bound it with a strip of rawhide and buried it under a log with several layers of decomposing leaves.

When the leaves of cottonwood, or any deciduous tree, pile up at the base of a tree, and are wet down and compressed under the weight of snow, several layers of leaves, like the pages of a book, can be used like a blanket for covering. Now with the hide rolled tight with the fur inside, and the thick pile of leaves and branches, she felt it would be secure for several days until they returned. Satisfied, she retrieved the horses, packed up and with pemmican in hand, started her days quest to find her husband.

To The Overland Trail

Chapter Thirty-One

Eagle's Nest

JIM BECKWOURTH SAT AT the table with Eli Grantham and Lazarus Taylor. Both men were former soldiers in the Confederate army and after their discharge had come West to escape the war that still raged in the East. The hot cups of steaming coffee held in their hands had been 'flavored' with a shot of rum that Eli kept in an earthenware jug under the counter.

"So, Jim, headin' back to the mountains are ye?" asked Eli as he looked at the whiskered mountain man, noting the tangle of whiskers with the salt and pepper colors.

"Yup. After that cutthroat Chivington did what he done, I'm through with any o' them soljers. I'm goin' back to the mountains. I tell you, I'se plum tired of people! If it ain't them pillagin' Cheyenne and Arapaho, it's the cussed Army an' it's wannabe leaders. They're worse'n a bunch o' politicians, ever one of 'em jockeyin' for glory or sumpin'. Even ol' Chivington, who I thought would be alright what with his preachin' background, bein' a minister an' all, why he's the sorriest one o' the bunch! So, I'ma gonna go back to the mountains where all I gotta deal with grizzly bears an' snow storms!"

Eli took a deep draught of his hot totty and looked at the mountain man before him and nodding his head said, "I know whatchu mean. I got so tired o' them blasted officer's in the butternut and grey, none of 'em knowin' what they was a doin', that the first chance I got, I left it all behind me. An' Lazarus here, mulatto tho' he is an fightin' wit' da South, was muh best friend and we just decided to blazes with it all. If they wanna kill each other off for no good reason, then let 'em have at it!"

"Hear, hear!" cheered Lazarus as he lifted his cup as a toast to the comments.

"Well, what about all these here attacks by them dog soljers I been hearin' about? Ain'tchu fellas fearful of an attack?" inquired the mountain man.

"No more'n anythin' else," declared Eli. "If the cold don't getcha, or some o' them road agents, then it's gonna be Injuns. But ol' Lazarus an' me was marksmen fer the boys in grey an' we keep a purty good eye out."

"Well, you know somebody's comin' up on you right now?" said Beckwourth with his voice lowered to just over a whisper.

"What? Where?" asked a startled Lazarus.

"Near as I can make out, two horses comin' down the road, 'bout 50 yards out," explained Beckwourth with a hand behind one ear as he looked in the direction of the roadway. Lazarus stepped to the front window, the small cabin had one window in the front and one by the back door to watch the corrals, and standing to the side, looked up the road to see a rather small figure in buckskins and a Hudson's Bay capote astraddle a long-legged sorrel and leading a pack horse.

"Ain't no Injun! Looks like a little feller in one o' them blanket coats," declared Lazarus. He stepped through the door and stood before the cabin with his Springfield cradled loosely in his arms to watch the visitor come closer. When the capot-clad visitor reined up the sorrel, Lazarus instructed, "Put yo' horses in the corral roun' back and come on in for some coffee."

He noted the dog on the horse's rump and the youthful face of the rider and motioned to the back of the cabin as the visitor gave a nod and kneed the sorrel toward the corrals.

Ginny motioned for Smokey to jump down and swung her leg over the cantle of her saddle to drop to the ground. It was easier for her to slide down the fender leathers than to try to stretch her leg to reach her landing. Once on the ground, she opened the gate and led her horses into the corral, loosened the cinches and led them to the water trough.

There was a sizable stick leaning on the back of the trough and she used it to break the ice for the horses to drink. Slipping her Henry from the scabbard and grabbing her saddlebags, she started for the back-door where Lazarus now stood. He stepped back into the cabin and held the door until she entered and he motioned her to the table. "Go 'head on a have a seat thar. That big feller's muh partner, Eli, and that mountain man lookin' one's named Jim, and I'm Lazarus. I'll git 'nother cup."

Ginny nodded her head to the men at the table, sat her rifle and saddlebags against the wall and started undoing her capote. When she pushed back the hood it took her knit cap with it and her long hair fell loosely to the side. Both men at the table looked with wide eyes, and Beckwourth said, "Why, yore a woman!"

"Figured that out, didja?" replied Ginny as she removed her capote revealing her buckskin tunic and the beaded belt that held her Colt in the holster and the tomahawk in her belt. "And heeled too! Now what's a woman doin' out here in this country, in this weather, and with Injuns all about?" asked Jim.

"Come to fetch my husband," said Ginny as she sat at the table and reached for her cup of coffee. "He's the Shotgun on the Overland stage and he's overdue. I figured he got in some trouble, so I set out to fetch him back home," she stated matter-of-factly, taking a sip of the dark brew. Eli lifted the jug of rum and with a nod of his head asked if she wanted some. She held out her cup and watched as he poured a tad into the coffee. She had been chilled to the bone and was willing to do whatever it took to get the warmth inside. She watched as the men, speechless, looked to one another and at her.

"Well, girl, you got gumption, I'll give you that. Not much sense, but gumption," said Eli as he wrapped his hands around the steaming cup before him.

"Now is that any way to talk to a woman, Eli?" reprimanded Lazarus. "Cain't yo' tell she's worried 'bout her man?"

"An' if he knew she was here, he'd be worried 'bout her! Now, let me ask you sumpin' missy, when yore husband left home, did he tell you to wait for him?"

"Yes, he did. But, he didn't tell me to wait at the cabin. And when the Indians took me, he came after me. So, I figured I should do the same."

"The Indians took you?" asked Eli incredulously.

"That's right. They took me and my friend and her little brother. And as soon as Talon found out about it, he came a high-tailin' it after us, and he didn't even know us at the time."

"Well, obviously, he got you back. How 'bout your friends?" asked Beckwourth.

Ginny took another sip and looked at the dark-skinned mountain man and replied, "He got us all back, safe and sound. So, you see, I just hafta get him back too!" she implored.

"Wait a minute, I remember that. That was just last year, weren't it? An' you all came through here on the stage, I remember. Let's see now, don't tell me, his name was uh . . .uh. . . Thomas!"

"Thompsett. Talon Thompsett and I'm Ginny Thompsett."

"Thompsett? That's an uncommon name. I met a fella a few years back, Independence I think it was, name o' Caleb, Caleb Thompsett. He was takin' a bunch o' buffler hunters out to the plains an' a couple o' his trouble makers left him and hooked up with me. Thot they'd have it easier with my outfit an' they was wrong 'bout that."

Ginny grinned and said, "That's Talon's daddy. He has a ranch up in the Medicine Bow, now."

"You don't say? Why, it shore is a small world, ain't it," declared Beckwourth as he stood up and strolled to the window. He looked out the distorted glass from the side, moved his head for a better look and said, "We got comp'ny!" in such a way that everyone knew it was trouble. Without discussion, Eli and Lazarus quickly removed the framed glass from the window openings and closed the shutters with their firing slots. Lazarus explained, "We sent all the way to St. Louie for dis glass, an' ain't gonna let no Injun shoot it out!"

The men had cut firing slots in the window shutters and in the door. On the off-side of the door and the opposite walls, they had also cut firing slots that were normally stuffed with rags, but were now removed. Jim stood at the window and Eli at the door. Lazarus took the firing slot on the off-side and as he started to put his Springfield through the slot, he instructed Ginny, "You take the back-window missy, them Injun's'll try to get to the horses. If you can shoot that thar Henry, you keep 'em away from the horses!" She nodded her head and took her position.

To The Overland Trail

Chapter Thirty-Two

Defending

ROMAN NOSE SPLIT HIS force letting Walks with Bear take a band of twenty and make for the Eagle's Nest station. He sent a band of forty to return to the village with the plunder and captives from the American Ranch and he remained behind with the rest, numbering about forty warriors, to take the Orchard station. Walks with Bear led his warriors to the bluff South of the Eagle's Nest station and gathered his chosen leaders to his side. He gave instructions to Crow to take three warriors and work their way through the trees along the river bank and come up behind the buildings of the station. Their task was to free the horses from the corral while the attack, led by Walks with Bear and Coyote Killer would come at the front.

The log cabin of the Eagle's Nest Station had a sod roof and solid walls giving the defenders excellent cover. The firing slots gave just enough space for the shooters to find their targets and protection as well. Beckwourth watched the Indians split into two groups and he knew they would alternate their charge. Repeating rifles were still too new to be widely used and the Indians expected the first charge to draw the initial fire and while the defenders were reloading, the second charge would bring a quick victory. But these were seasoned fighters that prepared for the attack and Beckwourth opened the ball with his big Sharps.

Walks with Bear held his men at a distance he judged out of range of the white man's rifles, about four hundred yards. He sat astride his war pony higher up the side of the bluff where he could survey the area before him and direct the battle. He lifted his lance to signal his warriors as the big Sharps boomed from the window of the cabin. The black war pony of the war leader stumbled forward and Walks with Bear fell over the withers and to the ground in front of the fallen horse. He scrambled up quickly and raising his lance signaled for the attack to begin.

Coyote Killer's band surged forward raising their lances and rifles, taunting the white men as they screamed their war cries. The band spread out and the Springfield's of Eli and Lazarus boomed and two warriors were knocked from their horses to be trampled by the others behind them. Beckwourth had mastered the falling block action of the Sharps and quickly reloaded a paper cartridge and before the charging Dog soldiers had advanced twenty yards, his smoke pole thundered from the firing slot and another warrior crossed over to meet his ancestors.

Ginny was startled by the big blast from the first shot of Beckwourth and jumped slightly, turned to see him reloading and heard the two quick shots of Eli and Lazarus as she turned back to watch through the firing slot of the back-window shutters. She caught a glimpse of what she thought was an Indian at the corner of the barn and she unconsciously drew a breath and held it, waiting for a shot.

The barrel of the Henry protruded from the firing slot and moved ever so slightly as she directed it to the barn, waiting. She expelled her breath and drew another just as the crouching Indian moved along the corral toward the gate to take the horses. Ginny squeezed off her shot and the Henry belched death dropping the Cheyenne. Her shot startled another sneak-thief and the movement caught Ginny's eye. She was quick to jack in another round and take aim and delivered the same message causing that Cheyenne to jerk up and backwards as blood blossomed on his chest.

Quickly jacking in another round, she searched the expanse of corral, knowing her sorrel and Talon's grulla were there and would be prime targets for the horse stealing Cheyenne. Taking slow breaths and trying to still her nerves, she watched. The constant booming of the men's rifles rattled every cup, plate and pan on the crude shelves, dropping some to the floor and further jarring Ginny's nerves, but she maintained her vigil.

Then she saw another warrior crouched at the corner of the corral and looking toward the cabin. His rifle barrel rested on one of the poles of the fence and she saw the barrel jump and smoke almost at the same instant the bullet nicked the log by the window and slammed into the shutter beside her. She jumped but quickly looked through the port and drew a bead as the warrior stood up slightly to see if he had succeeded in killing the shooter at the window. The bullet from the Henry pierced his eye and exploded from the back of his skull, driving the warrior to the ground never to move again.

Eli and Lazarus were skilled at the reloading of the Springfield and when battling together, would get into a rhythm. One would be firing while the other reloaded and between the two of them they would usually get off three shots each or six shots per minute. While Beckwourth could do as many as six shots per minute with his paper cartridges, the three men, exceptional marksmen all, dealt death at a terrible toll for the attackers.

The cabin became stifling with little ventilation and considerable smoke, yet with the muzzles outside the firing ports, the greater cloud of smoke was outside the cabin and hindered the attackers aim. The Sharps had an effective range of 500 yards and the Springfields in the hands of experienced marksmen had an effective range of 300 yards. The deadly accuracy of the defenders kept the Indians at a distance and the frustrated and angry Walks with Bear, now astride a commandeered war pony, shouted at his warriors commanding them to attack again.

The field of fire in front of the cabin was littered with bodies of dead and wounded and still they came. But the screaming war cries dissipated when more warriors fell and the tide of attackers turned away.

Beckwourth said, "I think we turned 'em boys. Looks like they be makin' for wide open yonder."

Eli and Lazarus slumped back to the chairs away from the walls and breathed deeply in relief. Eli looked at Lazarus and asked, "You okay?"

"Yup. You?"

Without answering, Eli turned to look at the woman at the back wall and saw her still standing and staring out the firing port. He asked, "Any more Injuns out back there, Missy?"

Without turning away from her slot, she answered quietly, "Only dead ones."

Eli rose from his seat and walked to her side and said, "Lemme have a look-see."

He peered through the slot, opened the shutters and looked to see the three dead Cheyenne would-be horse thieves. He scanned the area for any other sign and turned back to Ginny and said, "You done good, girl. Yessir, you done good."

Eli walked across the packed dirt floor to Beckwourth's side, who now craned to view the battleground before them as Eli said, "The girl kilt three o' them red devils."

Beckwourth looked at Eli and back at Ginny, now seated at the table and said to Eli, "She did? Three of 'em?"

Eli nodded his head and looked at the surprised expression of the seasoned mountain man and said, "Didja ever hear the like?"

Beckwourth shook his head and went to the table and said, "You'll do to ride the river with, Ginny. And if you'll let me, I'd be proud to come with you to look fer your man."

Ginny lifted her head to look at the grizzled man and said, "Uh, sure, that'd be fine. I could use the help, thanks. But right now, I need some more coffee, how 'boutchu?" and rose to fetch the coffee pot.

Before leaving, Ginny and Beckwourth shared a meal with the two friends that were now bound by blood. Anytime men, and in this case a woman as well, share a battle against a common foe, a bond of camaraderie is sealed that is never known by those that never experience life on the very edge of death.

The relief was apparent on the part of each one and stories were told and laughter shared while they enjoyed the simple but ample meal of deer steak smothered in gravy and sopped up with sourdough bread. As Ginny and Jim rode from the cabin, Eli and Lazarus stood side by side and waved at their departing friends.

To The Overland Trail

Chapter Thirty-Three

Orchard

ORCHARD STATION WAS AN established trading post long before the Overland Stage started its mail route through the territory. Davis and his wife, Clarice, were considered old-timers in this country and were well known among the Cheyenne and Arapaho. Many were the times when the sandy flats around the post looked more like an Indian village than a trading post. Davis had always treated the Indians with respect and was honest and fair in his dealings. The buildings were well built of thick logs and sod roofs. The main building served as the trading post and was the largest of the three, holding a long counter for bickered dealings, shelves and cabinets for goods, and a table and chairs for those customers who chose to imbibe before leaving.

Davis was a thick built man that resembled a stump more than a man, squatty with arms as big as large branches and legs like gnarled roots. His mutton chop whiskers were almost white and what hair was left was streaks of grey and white. A scar gave his nose an unnatural bend as it traveled across his cheek and disappeared into his whiskers. His eyes were grey and always moving, taking in everything and always judging. Under the counter lay a sawed-off double-barreled shotgun, loaded with anything deadly he found at hand. His oft repeated phrase of, "I didn't live this long bein' no fool," told of his character and demeanor.

Big Crow and Neva had both told Roman Nose of the well-stocked trading post and he was determined to bring those supplies to the village for his people. The many raids that had effectively wiped out the stage line and nearby ranches had netted them many cattle and the raid on Julesburg brought several wagon loads of other goods, but when the council had gathered the other bands from outside of Colorado territory, their numbers had increased dramatically and the needs were greater than ever.

He had been told by Big Crow that most of the Sioux, both Brule and Lakota, and the Arapaho, would be going North away from this territory and they would need additional supplies for the long journey. This trading post and station would provide most of what they lacked, if Roman Nose could take it and capture the supplies.

Davis had chosen this apparent desolate location because it was wide open in all directions. The only remnants of trees stood like a forest of skeletons grasping at the passing clouds with outstretched grey boney arms and fingers. The alkali and sand gave little purchase for any blown in seeds of any grass or shrubbery and the only time anything alive or moving was seen was if a strong wind blew in stray leaves or tumbleweeds.

But Davis was more concerned about defense than landscaping. He also knew most Indians coveted horses, but because of the deep sand, the stage line used mules that were better at pulling the heavy coaches through the loose sand, and most Indians had little interest in mules. For that reason, Davis didn't even keep horses for his own use, choosing instead to ride a mule whenever the need arose.

Roman Nose personally scouted the station in the grey light of early morning and now sat with his leaders well back beyond the sand hills. The report from Walks with Bear and the attack on Eagle's Nest had been disappointing and he angrily dispatched the decimated band to return to the villages. More determined than ever to show the whites the superiority of the natives, Roman Nose detailed the plan of attack.

Eagle Feather took ten men with him and circled wide around the station and came at the river well upstream. Almost two miles upriver, where the sand hills and flats gave way to richer soil and ample trees, the first band freed logs from a driftwood pile at the point of a small island. The logs were pushed into the current with men hanging on both sides. The only way to get near the post was by water and obscured from the view of the station by the riverbanks.

As they neared the station, they pushed the logs to the shore and clambered a short way up the bank and continued their preparations. With flint and steel, Eagle Feather started a small fire while the other men prepared what would become flaming arrows by wrapping the heads with trade cloth saturated with pine pitch. When all was ready, he gave the signal by sending an arrow aloft for Roman Nose to begin.

One man had been sent as scout to a small cluster of dead sagebrush and tumbleweeds and he now launched his arrow for Roman Nose to see. He motioned for Bear Claw to take his men forward. With Bear Claw in the lead, four warriors followed him toward the cabin. They rode forward leisurely and with one man carrying a small bundle of pelts as if they were on a trading mission.

Davis spotted the group of five warriors approaching, noticed they were without war paint and thought this was just another bunch of Indians wanting to trade for trinkets and geegaws. He spoke to two men at the table, "We got comp'ny comin', looks like five Cheyenne comin' to trade." The men nodded their heads in understanding, pulled their rifles near and continued to sip the hot brew. Davis walked behind the counter, checked his shotgun and cocked the hammers before laying it back on the shelf under the counter but within easy reach. He leaned on the counter with both elbows and waited.

Two men waited at the hitchrail while Bear Claw and the warrior with the pelts and Running Fox walked into the trading post. "Mornin'," greeted Davis and the Indians responded with grunts.

Bear Claw was surprised to see two buckskin clad whiskered men sitting at the table and nursing cups of coffee. Standing Elk lay the pelts on the counter and motioned to the clay jugs of trade whiskey on the shelf. Davis and the Indians knew he was not supposed to sell whiskey to the Indians and he never did, he didn't even like trading it to the trappers and pilgrims that passed through, his religion forbade it, but he saw the profit as more appealing than obedience to his religion. After all, who would know what he did way out here by himself. But he had always drawn the line at selling liquor to the Indians and was surprised one would ask for it now.

Davis shook his head no and pointed to a small barrel of beads and the shelf of other trade goods. Bear Claw stepped to the counter and shook his finger toward the jugs and shouted, "Whiskey! Now!" Davis let his hands drop below the counter and continued to shake his head and said just as loudly, "No! You can't have whiskey!"

Bear Claw grabbed at the knife at his waist and reached for the trader but Davis leaned back just far enough to escape his grasp and with the shotgun still under the counter, pulled a trigger, moved the sawed-off just a bit and pulled the other trigger. The explosions came so close together it sounded like on massive boom and rocked the shelves, causing some items to fall to the floor. The men at the table jumped to their feet and before Running Fox could react, he was shot through the chest by the Hawken held in the trapper's hands.

The shotgun blast tore through the thin curtain hanging from the counter to splatter the shot, glass, and gravel across the belts of both Bear Claw and Standing Elk, ripping open their midriffs so that when they were splayed on the hard-packed dirt floor, their entrails sought escape from their bellies and the pooling blood. The second trapper stepped quickly to the door and shot one of the two waiting warriors, causing the other to jerk the head of his mount around and slam his heels to its sides in his hurry to escape.

The explosion of gunfire was the signal for Roman Nose to attack, but it was supposed to be gunshots from his men, not the trader and trappers. But the attack was on, nonetheless. Davis and one of the trappers, known as Micky, quickly pulled the bodies of the three slain Indians out of the post and as they returned, Davis said, "Don't want them carcasses stinkin' up the place. Grab that Spencer you was wantin' from the shelf and have at 'er!"

The other trapper, Smith, was already closing the shutters and the door and reached for his big Sharps while his partner loaded his new Spencer.

Davis also grabbed and loaded another Spencer and stepped to the shuttered window to the left of the door. Smith took the door and Micky took the window to the right of the door. Because of the wide-open flats, the Indians had assembled beyond the sand hills that lay over five hundred yards distant. As the horde rounded the low rising hills, the defenders were ready for them and opened fire laying down a deadly fusillade.

Unseen from inside the post, Bear Claw signaled his men to release their flaming arrows against the buildings. Mrs. Davis, alone in the cabin behind the trading post, was the only one to see the arrows strike the post. Her first thought was to try to use her bucket of water and douse the arrows, but quickly realized she needed to protect herself and started shuttering the windows and barring the door.

She heard arrows striking the logs of the cabin and she ran for her bedroom to retrieve her Walker Colt. She sat down at the table, nervously rose to her feet when she heard the booming of the rifles from the post and stepped to the windows to peer through the firing slots to try to see what was happening. The smoke from the arrows obscured her view and she sat back at the table. She was nervous, and rightly so, as she heard the screams of the charging Indians. She saw the coffee pot, stood and poured herself a cup, sat back down and dropped her head to her hands then slipped her hands to her ears, trying to muffle the war cries.

Inside the post, the men kept a steady round of firing with ample ammunition readily at hand. Smith used a tube to load his Spencer and said, "My barrel's gettin' so hot I'm afeered it's gonna catch the window sill on fire!"

"Mine too," responded Micky as he slipped another paper cartridge into his Sharps.

"Oh, quitchur bellyachin' and keep shootin'! I'm thinkin' they done set fire to the place anyhoo!" said Davis between booms from his Spencer. "Lookee back yonder!" he said, motioning with his head to the back of the post. Smoke was snaking through the loose chinking between the logs and under the eaves.

"If we don't turn 'em back, we're gonna be worse off'n pig in a poke!" observed Smith.

"I shore didn't think that cup of hot coffee was worth all this!" replied Micky as he stuck his Sharps back through the firing slot. It soon boomed and bucked as another Cheyenne lost his bid for glory.

Clarice Davis bounced and flounced from her chair to the window and back to the chair. When there were no gunshots coming from the cabin, Bear Claw's men were emboldened and charged the rear of the buildings and two men now stood at the front door of the cabin. Clarice had just sat back down, when the banging of rifle butts on the door caused her to emit a scream, knowing the Indians were about to break in.

She spun her chair around and faced the door with the big Colt tightly gripped in both hands. She cocked the hammer and readied herself. The door slammed open and framed a big warrior with a beaded buckskin tunic, war paint of white streaks across the bridge of his nose extending to his ears, a broad grin that showed brown teeth, braids hanging on his shoulders with feathers in them and an old trade fusil rifle in his hands. The Colt roared and jumped in Clarice's hands. The grin disappeared as the warrior looked at the blood coming from his chest and as his knees gave way, slumped to a heap in the doorway. The warrior behind him screamed and raised a tomahawk as he started to step over the body of the first warrior but was stopped when the Walker Colt spat another slug that took him in the throat.

Clarice froze as she looked at the bodies lying in her doorway, saw the back of the post consumed in flames and looked around her to see smoke coming into the cabin from the back and side walls. She looked back to the door and saw other warriors approaching. She screamed in fear, sobbed and looked at the Colt in her lap. Another glance to the door at the warriors just steps away and she put the barrel of the Colt under her chin, paused and thought about her husband, and pulled the trigger.

The smoke began to fill the post and the men were choking when Smith asked, "Is there any way we can get outta here?"

"No, the back's all aflame, cain't get out there, mebbe we can sneak out the winders, but I doubt it," answered Davis.

"Go 'head on an' try, we'll keep shootin' an' cover you as much as we can. If'n you make it, find some place to give us cover an' we'll try it," shouted Smith.

Davis cracked open the shutters of the side window, and the cloud of smoke surrounding the post made it difficult to see, but also difficult to be seen. He hollered back, "O.K., I'm goin'!" and did a hop to lift himself to the window sill, leaned out the window and began pushing with his foot between the logs, but suddenly a tomahawk was buried in the side of his head.

His loud grunt caused Smith to look and step to the window in time to see the attacker reach for his hawk to retrieve it, but Smith's Spencer boomed and the attacker's head exploded. Smith quickly hoisted Davis' carcass through the window and closed the shutters. He told his partner, "It's just us'ns now. Davis is done fer." Micky's Sharps boomed again.

The smoke was too much to bear as Micky turned to Smith and said, "I ain't stayin' here to become roast pork! I'd rather be a pincushion fer Dog soljer arrers and die like a man. You with me?"

"Let's go!" shouted Smith.

Micky reloaded his Sharps, Smith jacked another round, and nodding at one another, Micky led the way. The door slammed open and both men ran through the cloud of smoke. Micky saw a charging Cheyenne, stopped and took aim and blew the warrior plum off the back of his mount.

Smith heard the scream of a war cry from his right, spun in that direction and fired his Spencer from his hip and dropped an Arapaho that was set on killing the white man with his tomahawk raised. Smith jacked another round, looked for a target and felt the first arrow pierce his chest, followed quickly by two more, then another. On his knees, he dropped his rifle at his side, looked to see Micky already on his back with several arrows in his body, and fell into the pit of darkness.

Chapter Thirty-Four

Searching

AS THEY LEFT EAGLE'S Nest station, James Beckwourth suggested to Ginny that the two of the them stay close to the tree line to take advantage of any cover. "What with them Dog sojers takin' a beatin' back at station, they might be hangin' back an' waitin' to hit any of us trav'lers," drawled the big mountain man. The cold wind of late morning prompted both to hunker down in their coats and pull their collars and scarves up around their ears. "That consarned wind feels worse'n one o' them Injuns scalpin' knives, whooooeeeee!" Their horses walked with heads drooped in protest of the wintry morning, but their shuffling gait stirred the dust of the roadway around their hooves only to have it quickly dissipated by the ground hugging wind.

Just over an hour on the trail and Smokey came running back to Ginny, obviously upset as he growled and yipped as he ran back and forth before the horses. Ginny said, "He's upset about something, we better move back in the trees," as she reined her horse into the scattered cottonwoods. Tall thick willows gave visual cover but weren't enough for cover in a fight. As Beckwourth swung a leg over his horse's rump, he paused as he heard the volley of gunshots from the direction of Orchard station.

He motioned to Ginny to dismount and taking the leads of all three horses, he led them into a thicker grove of cottonwood and alder. He tied off the horses and slipped his Sharps from the scabbard, motioning for Ginny to get her Henry. He motioned for her to take cover behind a pile of driftwood and knelt beside her, keeping his eyes on the tree-line that separated them from the clearing and the distant station. As they listened, the gunfire tapered off and they could see the rising smoke from the station buildings. Occasionally the wind would carry the sounds of screamed war cries as the Indians pillaged the trading post and station.

Beckwourth looked at Ginny and dropped his eyes as he realized the woman before him was thinking of her missing husband and was fearful he might be at that station. He shook his head slowly from side to side and whispered, "There's nothin' we can do. Way I figger it, this is a different bunch than attacked us and quite a few more of 'em too. We'll just have to wait till they're gone, then we'll check it out."

She nodded her head in acceptance, dropped back and seated herself on the sand, pulled Smokey beside her and lay her Henry across her lap to wait. Beckwourth seated himself beside her and said, "Tell me about him, what'd you say his name was, Talon?"

She grinned as she started, "Talon. He's a twin to Tyrell, but I got the best one. He's taller'n you, broad shouldered, good looking and the best man I've ever known. He's good at anything he does, riding, shooting, chasin' Indians, you name it, he can do it. And he's not afraid of anything! Why, when I shot that bear, he came a runnin' and woulda charged that bear with his Arkansas Toothpick, if he wasn't already dead, but he came anyway."

"Wait a minute, the bear you shot? You shot a bear?"

"Yup, had to, he didn't wanna get outta the way an' I had to go get the horses," she said, pleading for understanding.

"And he didn't even know us when we were taken by those Cheyenne Dog soldiers, and he came after us, all by his lonesome, anyway. Now, that's a man, wouldn't you say?"

"Uh, yeah, I reckon," replied Beckwourth as he thought, *And you're some kinda woman, too!*

He motioned for her to be still and quiet as he looked over the driftwood pile and watched the departing Indians. They had commandeered the wagon from the barn, loaded it to overflowing with plunder from the trading post and were leaving. They chattered excitedly among themselves as their horses trudged through the loose sand to make their way to the far bluffs and easier traveling along the bluffs away from the sandy river bottom.

After waiting most of an hour before moving, Beckwourth and Ginny rode to the still smoldering buildings of the Orchard station. Ginny moved her knit scarf to cover her mouth and nose as she was met with the stench of burning flesh. As they neared the first pile of rubble, the mutilated bodies of the two trappers lay near one another. The arrows had been plucked from their bodies, but they had been robbed of their britches, moccasins, and scalps.

At first sight of the buckskins, Ginny was startled and afraid one of them might be Talon but was relieved to see both men were much older. Beckwourth noticed the droop of her shoulders as she recognized they were not her man and he let a slight grin of relief cross his wrinkled face. "You wait here, and I'll have a look around," said Beckwourth as he handed her the reins of his horse. He made a quick survey, noticed the partially burned body of Davis, saw the remains of Clarice in the still smoldering cabin and the body of the hostler, mutilated beyond recognition, at the doorway to the barn, then returned to Ginny's side.

"Well, since he's not here, I guess we keep lookin'," stated the old trapper as he took one last look at the devastation. "I figger that as long as we don't see any sign of a stage, then we'll just keep lookin', whatsay?"

"Yeah, I reckon you're right. He wouldn't leave the stage unless there was a fight or sumpin' an' then he'd have to have sum'thin' to ride. You don't think we could miss him, do ya?" she asked the old-timer.

"Not unless he's shyin' mighty wide of the road and the river, an' I don't think he'd be doin' that. It gits mighty cold out there in them flats and he wouldn't have no cover, neither," stated the mountain philosopher.

He swung aboard his mount and motioned for Smokey to lead off as they followed the roadway, such as it was. There were still some planks and logs that showed from under the drifting sand and snow, leftover from the attempt by the line to make a better roadway through the deep sand. An attempt that was unsuccessful and left as much of a hindrance as a help to the passing coaches. Beckwourth twisted to look behind him at the descending sun and tried to calculate how much daylight remained. He knew they would need to make camp soon but there was nothing nearby. He asked Ginny, "Have you been thisaway before? Know anythin' about the road?"

"Just once, and I really wasn't paying much attention to the surroundings. We were too busy watchin' for Indians. But I think 'bout where the trees show up along the bank, there's some caves or sumpin' back along the bank. I remember them 'cuz they were so unusual."

"I ain't mucha one fer caves n' such, but if there's trees, we'll find us a place to camp. We got time yet, so we'll do alright," he assured her.

Talon felt better with some meat in his belly, but his mind began to work about the Indians. He had heard enough to know they were headed to the Orchard station and it was too far and they were too many for him to be of help. But after they attacked the station, they would probably return the same way they traveled before and that would put him right in the path of their return. As he considered the possibilities, whether to return to his leaf covered lair beneath the downed cottonwood, retreat to his overhang shelter that provided little camouflage, or leave, he easily chose leaving.

The terrain between his present location and the Orchard station was wide open after leaving the nearby trees. He wouldn't be able to travel across the sandy roadway and there would be little or no cover. The distant bluffs and sand hills were too far and too sparse to give any protection. He looked at the riverbank and recalling previous trips, knew the riverbank, at this time of year, was six to eight feet above water level and often held clusters of willows that could provide enough cover to hide. If it came to a battle, the only cover would be the riverbank but that was certainly more than the occasional snag of dead trees across the alkali and sand flats before the Orchard station.

He shuffled to the overhang to retrieve his buffalo robe and haversack of supplies, meager though they were. He thought about his Henry and considered looking for it, but knew his splinted leg would keep him from maneuvering the rocks of the hillside with the scattered debris and time was limited. He would like to have his Henry and thought it would be better than the Spencer in a close fight, but given the choice of his scalp and the Henry, he was pretty certain his scalp would keep him warmer.

With one last quick survey, he slipped the strap of the haversack over his shoulder, draped the buffalo robe over the same shoulder and with Spencer in hand, he grabbed his crutch and started toward the river bank. He struggled to sit on the edge of the bank then slid down to the gravel, catching himself with his bum leg and wincing in pain. He awkwardly rose to his feet, stooped to pick up his gear, and with the Spencer hanging from the fashioned sling, started negotiating his way on the gravel bar alongside the ice shelf of the river. He made about two miles, stumbling along with the gravel crunching underfoot, before he sat down on a stump of driftwood for a short rest. He noticed the smoke drifting along the waterway and knew it had to be from the Orchard station attack and he shook his head as he thought of the folks that kept the station and trading post.

He heard the creak of a wagon and carefully looked over the edge of the bank to see the party of Indians trailed by the stolen wagon full of plunder. He dropped his head and looked about him for any cover and there was none. He froze in place, not wanting to even breathe for fear of giving himself away. Against so many he would have no chance of escape or survival; his only hope was that they would pass on by. He waited and listened, craning to hear any sound beyond the chuckling of the river behind him. He watched as the shadows on the far bank lengthened with the setting of the sun.

With the light fading, he moved up the bank to get a view of the open flats before him. It was empty and he breathed a sigh of relief at the emptiness. He searched the distant tree-line downstream for any sign of life and finding none decided to continue his troublesome trek to give more distance between him and the Dog soldiers.

Just before dark, he approached a thick cluster of willows and knew it would be the best cover and shelter he would find. Usually in thick groves of willows like these, there were tunnel-like overhangs formed by the passage of many small animals and it was into one of these the crippled Talon crawled. Well within the overhanging branches, he maneuvered for a comfortable sleeping space, rolled out his buffalo robe and after chewing some of the tough raw remnants of the deer carcass, dropped off to sleep.

Ginny motioned to Beckwourth toward a growth of alder and willows at the edge of the riverbank. It was the only cover available and the mountain man nodded his head in agreement. They nudged their horses over the edge of the bank to a sand bar at water's edge.

Ginny hobbled her horses and Beckwourth followed suit. Speaking in a low voice he said, "We better have a cold camp tonite, what with them Injuns so nearby, don't wan'em smellin' smoke an' go to nosin' around."

Ginny replied with a "Ummhummm," as she dug into her parfleche for the remains of the roast and sourdough bread. There would be just enough for the two of them to stave off hunger for the night.

To The Overland Trail

Chapter Thirty-Five

Discovery

IT HAD BEEN A restless night. The cluster of willows did little to keep out the cold wind along the river bottom and it seemed to aggravate the leg injury. Talon turned on his side, pulled his legs toward his chest and wrapped himself in the buffalo robe. It was usually enough to dispel the cold and retain the warmth of his body, but as the wind whistled through the willows and the cold rose from the frozen ground, it was hard to sleep.

Well before first light, he crawled from his lair and started back upstream, struggling with his gear, robe and crutch. Accustomed to moving silently, he found it difficult to maneuver along the rocky space between the rise of the riverbank and the ice border of the river. He hoped that anyone hearing his passing would take it for the sound of hooves on stone of an animal searching for an early morning drink. The stars did little to light his way and the last quarter of the moon provided nothing but a symbol of hope.

Although his eyes were adapted to the darkness, and the starlight on the river donies and gravel kept him away from the water, he was nervous about the clatter of his crutch and the rolling of stones and searched for a path away from the gravel. He noticed what appeared to be a grassy area as the riverbank cut back toward the alkali flats. He started in the direction of the grassy knoll and at first was relieved as his moccasins whispered through the tall blades of grass. Although he could move quietly, dragging his legs through the tall grass was a struggle. He moved his good leg, then leaned forward to place his crutch and bad leg, then his good leg, and the crutch. But this time the crutch sunk into the soil or mud and he staggered and fell forward. The splash in the muck and mire and the feel of sharp edged blades that were bigger than grass made him realize he had fallen into a bog of cat-tails!

He thrashed around, trying to find footing and not lose his haversack or other gear and he wanted to yell in his frustration, but kept his silence, as much as possible, as he splashed in the muck. On his knees with water and mud almost to his waist, he reached out in the darkness feeling for his robe and haversack. There, there's the robe, and as he pulled it toward him, he felt the haversack floating beside it. Feeling for his crutch, he floundered around a moment or more until his hand fell on the sapling he had fashioned into his crutch. Driving the stick into the mud, he used it to stand but then struggled to free it from the muddy bottom. Finally, with crutch at his side and dragging the robe and haversack, he worked his way back the direction he came, thankful his sling held the Spencer on his back. *That's all I'd need is to lose my rifle!*

Smokey came to his feet with a low growl rumbling in his chest. Ginny rolled to her side and with one hand reaching for her Henry and the other on Smokey's back, whispered, "Easy boy, I heard it too. Somethin's out in a bog yonder. Maybe it's a deer comin' down to water. Let's just wait a bit an' see."

In the shadows of the night, she saw Beckwourth roll from his robes and rise to a crouch with rifle in hand. He looked at Ginny and was pleased to see she held her Henry. He whispered, "I'm gonna go see what's makin' that ruckus. Don't shoot me when I come back, ya hear?"

"Never you mind 'bout me, I only shoot bears an Injuns. Even though you do look like that bear I kilt, I won't shoot you."

He disappeared in the darkness as he made his way clear of the small grove. Knowing the only cover was the riverbank, he stealthily moved alongside the crumbling wall of clay and sand. Feeling his way more than seeing, he moved slower than a lazy turtle, maintaining a silence even as he felt the gravel and current smoothed stones underfoot. As he approached the bog, the first hint of the grey band of light along the Eastern horizon backlit the creature coming from the stand of cat-tails. At first the shadowy figure made him think moose, but when only the front shoulders, or what looked like shoulders, a big hump anyway, showed, he thought it might be a wounded buffalo. But he soon realized the struggling figure was a man.

Beckwourth cocked the hammer of his Sharps and knew the 'click-click' of metal would sound loudly in the still of early morning. The sound caused the figure to freeze and Beckwourth said just loud enough to be understood, "That's right, just stand steady right where you are," as he walked closer to the man. "Since there ain't 'nuff light to see much of you, how 'bout you tellin' me whatchur doin' sneakin' about."

"I ain't sneakin', blast it, I stumbled into that stinkin' bog, an' I got a broke leg an' it was hard gittin' out. Now who mightchu be?"

"I be James Beckwourth, an we be a huntin' a feller name o' Talon."

"Well, you found him."

Beckwourth stood tall and sat the butt of his Sharps on the ground beside him and as the morning light chased the darkness from the sky, he looked at the miserable figure before him. "Hummph, the way yore smellin' I ain't too sure I'm happy 'bout findin' you."

"Well, if you'll get a fire goin', I'll just walk out inta' that river and get shuck of some o' this mud."

"That thar sounds like a plum good idee, we're just up the river a short jaunt, an' thar's a backwater pool that'd be just right fer a mornin' bath. Come along, I'll help ya' a mite."

As they approached the camp, Beckwourth spoke out, "Hol' on thar, I'm comin' in with a mud dog I found back yonder. Don't shoot."

Ginny stepped from behind the alder brush with Henry in hand as she tried to make out the shadowy silhouette figures coming towards her. Beckwourth was easy to make out but the other one looked and smelled like some kinda swamp creature. The morning cold had driven her to her capote and she now pushed the scarf up around her nose to shield her from the smell. Recognizing the stripes at the bottom of the Hudson's Bay capote, Talon asked, "Ginny?"

She froze in fear that she was imagining what she heard and tentatively responded, "Talon? Is it you?" as the excitement began to build within her she took a step but Smokey beat her to his side and with wagging tail, jumped up on his leg and staggered him.

But when Talon answered, "It's me, alright," she ran forward, ignoring the smell and the muck of the mud and threw her arms wide and grabbing his shoulders, almost knocking him backwards, she started to kiss his muddy face and recoiled at the sight and smell and said, "Eewwwiiieee, you stink!" Then looking at his bewildered expression, she tiptoed up and kissed him anyway. As she drew back, he grinned at her muddy face and thought she was the most beautiful thing he'd ever seen.

Beckwourth gathered an armload of dry driftwood along the river shore and started a fire, bigger than usual, but with the long dead dry wood, there would be little smoke and what there was would be filtered in the branches of the cluster of trees and brush. Ginny knelt at the ice along the water's edge, splashed water on her face and hands to wash off the transferred mud

226

and watched Talon, sitting in the shallow backwater and splashing water on his chest and face, then rinse his robe and tunic. He tossed the robe and tunic to the gravel, struggled to his feet and asked, "Could you hand me that crutch?"

She eagerly stretched her hand with the crutch for him to grasp and watched as he shivered and struggled to shore. She was so happy she couldn't stop grinning and reached her arm around his waist to help him to the fire. She handed him her robe and instructed him to "Shuck it all, so we can dry it." He shivered as he wrapped up in the robe, shucked his britches and union suit, handed them to her and took a seat at the log beside the fire. He carefully stretched out his injured leg and knew it would have to be splinted and bound again, but it felt good to let it soak up the warmth of the fire.

Ginny put on a pot for coffee, passed out some strips of smoked meat and apologized, "Sorry we don't have anything better. We ate the last of what we had last night. But maybe we'll get some fresh meat today."

"This is mighty fine, I'm happy to be eatin' anything and smellin' that coffee, why, that's plum wonderful!"

They spent most of the morning drying out both Talon and his clothes and catching up on the events of the last several days. Ginny was saddened to hear about Bull and both Ginny and Beckwourth were surprised at the extent of the desolation of the Indian attacks. Talon was relieved to hear there had been no attacks, at least that they knew of, West of Eagle's Nest.

"But I think there's gonna be some, probably quite a few, before all this is over. The Cheyenne and Arapaho are still upset at what Chivington done, and rightly so, and they're out to show they don't like what the government's done by takin' away their land."

"Cain't rightly blame 'em none," stated Beckwourth. "There's just so blamed many pilgrims comin' out fer either gold or land, an' there ain't no stoppin' 'em."

227

"I couldn't hear everything that was said, but from what I could cipher, it sounds like most of 'ems headin' North with the Lakota."

"Ya don't say? Wal, if them Cheyenne and Arapaho join up wit' the Sioux, ya know the Brule and the Lakota, that'd be a bunch of Injuns allied together against the white man. An' with them numbers, there ain't no tellin' what they'll do. Don't think it's gonna be safe to travel in that part of the country. Mebbe I'll just hang 'round chere fer a spell," said Beckwourth.

When Eagle's Nest station came into view the sun was dropping behind the distant mountains but the Western sky was painted in brilliant hues of orange and gold, a fitting end to a rewarding day. Eli and Lazarus made the trio welcome and prepared a sumptuous meal of antelope steak, cat-tail roots, gravy and biscuits. When Talon and Jim shared the news of the other stations, Eli and Lazarus looked at one another as Eli asked his friend, "Ya think we oughtta get outta here or stay?"

"This is the only home we've known fer the last fo' year an' I ain't liken the idee of givin' it up to no Injuns"

"Okay then, we'll stay. You can pass word on to the line we're gonna need some more horses or mules but we be here!"

"We'll do that Eli, and proud to do it too. I don't reckon there'll be too many stages very soon, but knowin' you're here, I'm sure they'll be restocking soon 'nuff," answered Talon.

Choosing the hay of the barn over the cramped quarters of the station, Talon and Ginny rolled out their bedrolls and buffalo robes and spent the night huddled together and never left each other's clutches. They were awakened all too soon by the prying light of the rising sun and were soon back in the cabin and nursing their cups of coffee. Both Talon and Ginny were anxious to get home but Beckwourth said, "I'm thinkin' I'll stay shy of folks an' head up North. Mebbe do a little more trappin', mebbe find me 'nother Crow woman 'fore I have to spend 'nother winter by my lonesome."

Talon grinned at the wrinkled expression of the legendary mountain man and as he stretched out his hand to shake said, "I can't thank you enough for helping Ginny. We'll be forever in your debt."

"Nahsuh, it's me that'll be in debt to you two. It's been my pleasure to meet the both of ya and my life is the richer for it. You just be sure to take care of that thar girl, she's one to ride the river with, an' that kinda woman's mighty hard to find. You two'll be welcome at my fire anytime."

The men clasped hands, Ginny tiptoed and gave Jim a hug and said, "Thanks Jim, I'll never forget it!" He nodded his head and stepped back as she gave a hop to reach the stirrup and mounted up. Talon motioned for Smokey to lead out and put heels to his horse as the two left Eagle's Nest behind. The stage road hugged the tree line of the South Platte and the twelve miles to Latham were soon behind them. Although anxious to get home, the Latham hotel beckoned and a night in a feather bed proved irresistible.

To The Overland Trail

Chapter Thirty-Six

News

BEFORE LEAVING LATHAM, Talon and Ginny stopped at the stage station to share what they knew about the Indian assaults. With the telegraph lines down, this was the first news of the many attacks. Most folks were apprehensive of what was happening, but with no first-hand accounts, gossip and speculation fueled the fears. The division agent, Hugo Richards, came from the back room and listened intently as Talon told of the devastation. He shook his head and said, "Looks like it'll be a while 'fore we run any more coaches that direction. That's gonna take a lot of supplying of men, animals, and all the rest."

Talon was somewhat surprised at the agent's lack of regard for the many deaths of the station keepers and helpers, but knew the man's primary concern was for the stage line. "As far as I know, the only coach that was lost was the one we were on that took a tumble over the bank this side of Bijou Creek. Ain't nuthin' left of it, but there were some mail bags that might be salvaged."

"Hummm, yes, we'll have to do that. What about you? When will you be able to make a run?" asked the agent as he looked at the wrapped leg and crutch.

"Oh, it'll be a while yet. I'll keep in touch with the station at LaPorte, but I think we'll be takin' some time off, maybe go visit my family."

Ginny looked at her husband when he shared that with the agent. He had said nothing about making a trip to his family, but Ginny was pleased at the news. The thought of having him all to herself for a few days and then time with the family thrilled her and made her smile at her forced change of plans. *That'll be even better!* She thought as she kept her hand on her husband's arm and gave it a slight squeeze.

Richards instructed the telegraph operator to notify the other stations about the raids and to send one to Mr. Holladay as well. Although the telegraph was still in its infancy, towns and governments had become very reliant on the ability to quickly spread news and alarms. Richards knew the word would be passed to the troops at the many forts that had been established along the stage route for the protection of travelers and the stages and Holladay would demand action to be taken to ensure the safety of the mail carriers. He would have to confer with the other division superintendents and coordinate a rebuild and resupply of the many stations. He almost envied Talon's broken leg that would keep him out of service for some time.

They rode up the main street of LaPorte just as the sun dipped below the mountain tops. With a short stop for a meal at Aunt Sophie's and a quick visit with Mary Sue, they were soon on their way to the cabin. It would be so good to be home and both kicked their mounts to a trot to hasten their homecoming. Two very tired bodies struggled to get through the necessary chores. Talon tended the horses and gear, Ginny took the parfleche, saddle bags and rifles from the porch into the house and put things away. When Talon stepped through the door, bedrolls under his one arm and steadying himself on his crutch, Ginny smiled and walked to him and began to smother him with kisses. "Oh, it's so good to be back home. I thought this day would never come!"

"I know whatchu mean, for a spell there I wasn't too sure I'd make it home. But I'm sure glad I did," as he dropped the bedrolls and crutch to wrap her in his arms and pull her close and kiss her. He met no resistance and enjoyed the moment of shared love. She pushed back slightly to look at his whiskered face and said, "Just when did you decide about this visit to your family?"

"When I saw your smilin' face with the mud all over it! I thought you were so purty I knew I had to share you with my family. Even though they met you at the weddin', I just thought it'd be good for you to get to know them better and vice versa."

"Sounds wonderful, I'm excited about it. It'll be great to spend time away from all this Indian stuff. I'm kinda tired of all the killin' and such."

"Ummmhummm, but right now, I'm ready to call it a night."

They took an extra day to rest up and prepare for their journey, but both were anxious to get started and to see his folks. With an early start the following day, Talon chose to take the trail that led across the Medicine Bow foothills and dropped down near the headwaters of the North Platte. With one overnight stop, the easier trail followed the river and cut through the dark timber before they broke into a flat that overlooked the valley.

Talon reined up and waited for Ginny to ride up alongside. He rested one elbow on the pommel and nodded his head to the valley below. "There it is, ain't it pretty?"

"Oh, my yes! And I can just imagine how beautiful it would be in the springtime when everything's turning green. Even now with the snow in the trees and everything, it's beautiful."

"Yeah, I kinda miss it, but if I hadn't left, I'd never have found you!"

"Well, I'm glad you left. If you hadn't, no tellin' what woulda happened when those Indians had us. I probably wouldn't even be alive," she said somberly as she looked at her husband. He dropped his head at the thought of being without her and took a deep breath and said, "We better get on down there so we can make it in time for supper. I'm gettin' so hungry my belly button's pinchin' my backbone!"

Ginny giggled and dug her heels into the ribs of her sorrel and started on the trail at a canter, looked back at Talon as he slapped leather to catch up. When the trail dropped into the valley alongside the North Platte, they reined back to a walk and rode side by side as Talon pointed out different places and told the tales of his youth. As they rode up the trail to the cabin, he saw Caleb and Clancy standing side by side on the porch watching with curious stares to see who was coming to their cabin.

The instant of recognition painted a smile on his mother's face to be mirrored by the faces of Talon and Ginny. He heard a squeal of delight from his mother and a chuckle from his father as they came down the steps to greet the arriving couple.

"Boy, if you two aren't a sight for sore eyes! It is good to see you!" declared Caleb and he reached for the reins of his son's grulla. He looked at Ginny and said, "Git on down, I'll take care of the horses. You too, Talon, I'm sure your Ma is looking for some hugs or somethin',"

Ginny's feet had barely touched ground and she was wrapped in a bear hug by Clancy. The two women laughed and giggled and hugged some more. Clancy motioned to Talon to follow as the two women, arm in arm walked back up the steps to the porch and into the cabin. She hadn't noticed Talon's struggle and the crutch and was surprised when he hobbled into the cabin. She slapped her hands to her face and looking at Talon said, "What happened to you?" "Broke it, but it's healin' alright. We'll tell those stories later. Right now, I'm hungry, whatcha got to eat?"

"Oh you, always thinking about your stomach, you haven't changed a bit! Come on and sit down, I'll finish supper and you can eat to your heart's content." Ginny rose to help and the two women continued their chatter as Talon used an extra chair for his leg.

When Caleb came in and sat down at the table, he looked at his son and said, "So, you gonna tell us about it?" motioning to his leg. Talon began with the telling of all the happenings of the previous couple of weeks and concluded the story just as the women set the food on the table.

The four joined hands as Caleb asked the Lord's blessing on the meal and the time of visiting, thanking Him for bringing his son and wife home safely. As he said "Amen", Ginny added, "And there's something else," and grinned at Talon as she said, "We're having a baby!"

Talon was stunned at his wife's announcement, then struggled to his feet to grab his wife, now on her feet, and give her a big bear hug. Clancy reached for Caleb's hand and smiled at her grinning husband and said, "Whatchu think about that, Grandpa!?"

About the Author

Born and raised in Colorado into a family of ranchers and cowboys, B.N. is the youngest of seven sons. Juggling bull riding, skiing, and high school, graduation was a launching pad for a hitch in the Army Paratroopers. After the army, he finished his college education in Springfield, MO, and together with his wife and growing family, entered the ministry as a Baptist preacher.

Together, B.N. and Dawn raised four girls that are now married and have made them proud grandparents. With many years as a successful pastor and educator, he retired from the ministry and followed in the footsteps of his entrepreneurial father and started a successful insurance agency, which is now in the hands of his trusted nephew. He has also been a successful audiobook narrator and has recorded many books for several award-winning authors. Now finally realizing his life-long dream, B.N. has turned his efforts to writing a variety of books, from children's picture books and young adult adventure books, to the historical fiction and western genres which are his first love

Discover more great titles by B. N. Rundell and Wolfpack Publishing at:
http://wolfpackpublishing.com/b-n-rundell/

Made in the USA
Monee, IL
13 April 2021

65598606R00138